To Be A Mountain Man

Tom Franklin, driven by the lure of the west faces the challenge and danger of the frontier to become a mountain man.

James Oliver Virmala

Edition 2

Cover Photo By James Oliver Virmala

ISBN: 978-0-9972536-3-4

DEDICATION

In memory of a friend and project partner, Larry Northup, who brought me back to the world of the western frontier.

CONTENTS

BOOKS BY THE AUTHOR

Oli's Gold Book One
Search For Oli's Gold Book Two
Return To Oli's Gold Book Three
To Be A Mountain Man
Trouble On The Kansas Plains
Frontier Justice
Return Of The Mountain Man
The Tall Man
The Prospector
The Green Valley
Twilight Of The Mountain Man
The Mother Lode
Quest Of The Mountain Man
Journey's End
Rufus Pike
Rufus And The Pup
The Winding Trail Home
Rufus The Lost Years
The Kankakee Kid
Bogus Island
Tyler Tomas The Brothers' War
War of 1812 The Choice

ACKNOWLEDGMENTS

I would like to thank my good friend Barb who supplied guidance and encouragement during the writing of my books.

Thanks to Mark who edits my books. I appreciate his historical knowledge, which keeps me thinking and writing in the period of the story.

Thanks to the many friends who read the books and made me aware of needed corrections which help to make the writing error free. Even more important, sharing their favorite parts of the books, which is priceless to me.

CHAPTER ONE

It was early afternoon in April of 1839 when a tall man with light brown hair climbed out of the 30-foot cargo boat amidst the hustle and bustle of the St. Louis pier. There were four flat-bottomed, tall-sided boats that had traversed the Ohio and Mississippi Rivers from Buffalo New York, using push poles and oars to propel them through the churning spring waters.

The young man was Tom Franklin, one of the two Franklin brothers who had started on the trip, on their way to becoming mountain men. Tom's brother Isaac had been killed by an arrow to the throat while coming down the Ohio River. The strain of the trip, compounded by the loss of his brother, showed in the face of the tall man. He hardly noticed the steamships docked at the landing and the piles of goods that were transported to and from the pier.

He stood clutching two Kentucky long rifles and his bags. At the moment, Tom was unsure of where to go. For the last month, his every move had been directed by Henry Wilson, who owned the boats, or Boss Tuck, who was in charge of boat number four, which Tom had been assigned to.

St. Louis was the furthest Tom had ever been to the west, but he knew the mountains he hoped to trap in were still another thousand miles away. Never once had the young man thought that he would be making the trip alone. Hope surged through him as he saw Frenchy tossing packs to a young, blond-haired man who had been on the boat. Tom had heard him speak of going west.

The man was Oli August, and Tom had helped him get a job on the boats. Frenchy was kidding the young man about losing much of his pay to a red-headed woman at a landing along the Ohio. It had been Oli who was fighting alongside Isaac when he was killed. The brother had been buried in a cove not far from the skirmish, and Oli had made a crude marker for the grave, then had given Tom support in the following days.

Tom set his bags down and waited for the blond man to reach him. "I'm still going to the mountains," he said. "My brother and I dreamed of becoming trappers too long for me to give it up. I hear they have a rendezvous each year to sell furs and resupply. I plan on being at the one next spring. I would be honored if you would join me."

There was an awkward silence as Oli stood holding his gear. Finally, the blond man said, "As much as I'd like to, Tom, I can't go with you. I have something I have to do. Maybe if things don't work out, I'll come to the rendezvous and look you up."

The brown-haired friend understood. Not everyone's dream was to become a buffalo hunter or mountain man. Holding out Isaac's Kentucky long rifle, Tom said, "This was my brother's. I can only carry one rifle. I want you to have it."

The blond man was reluctant to take it and suggested he trade it for the Hawken he wanted. Tom, suddenly filled with emotion, thrust it into Oli's hands. Grabbing his packs, Tom turned and walked away. Without looking back, he said, "Goodbye, my friend, and safe trip."

Quickly losing himself in the crowds, Tom had never felt so alone. He walked blindly away from the pier. Two men suddenly stepped close to him, bumping him from both sides. He felt their hands grabbing at his gear and possible bag. Instinctively, Tom threw an elbow at one and struck the other with his rifle barrel. Both of the men ran away empty-handed.

The young man continued, almost running through the dusty streets of St. Louis, looking for someplace away from people. He saw the open doors of the livery. He hurried into it and dropped his bags onto the dusty wooden floor. Tom looked around the dim interior and noticed a man working in the back.

"I'll be right with you," the hostler called. "I jest got to get this stubborn mule in its stall."

Tom stood waiting, unsure of the past few moments. Had he been running from fear of the crowds, or had it been his past that he needed to escape from? It had been his dream to come west, and he had convinced Isaac to come with him. Before he left St. Louis, he would have to write the letter to their folks telling of the boy's death. Since the attack, Tom had been riddled with guilt.

His thoughts were interrupted by the approach of the stoop-shouldered, old hostler. The man gave him a wide, toothless grin. "What can I do for you, sonny?"

Needing someone to talk to, Tom leaned his rifle against the wall and sat down on a nail keg. "I come here to be a mountain man and don't know where to even start," he admitted. "I need someone to tell me what the next move should be, and . . . and I need a horse."

Immediately, Tom had the man's attention. "I can make some suggestions of who to talk to about hunting or trapping, although I've never been farther west than this here town. Now, as far at a horse, that I know I can help you with."

Feeling better just having acknowledged that he needed help, Tom stood up. "Show me what you've got."

The hostler led him toward the back. "Could I suggest a fine tempered mule? Now that's the kind of animal that'll take you to the Rockies and back."

"I heard you cussing the mule back there," Tom let him know. "I think I'll stay with a horse."

Following the man to a corral near the side, the hostler pointed to a horse working on a fork full of hay. "I can let you have that one for a good price."

"It kind of looks long in the tooth," Tom replied. "If this is all you got, I best start looking elsewhere."

Shaking his head, the hostler assured him, "You're looking at a good horse there, and you'll have a hard time finding horseflesh in St. Louis."

"Then I'll just have to start west on foot," the young man told him.

"Not so fast, sonny," the old man said, smiling. "I think I got just the animal for you."

Leaving the livery, the stoop-shouldered man led Tom up the street to a rundown, clap-board house with a sagging barn in the back. Pulling the low barn door open, he led him past a couple of milking cows to the back section of the building. The wall that divided the barn had a wide doorway with two poles across it.

To Tom's surprise, there were four nice-looking horses in box stalls. An open door to the left let in light and fresh air. Feeling some doubt, Tom told the man, "I assume you own these animals."

"Now hold on, sonny," the hostler cautioned him. "I am authorized to sell these horses."

"I take it you live here?" Tom asked.

"That I do, with my lovely wife, Esther," the old man replied. "She makes sweet butter and a fine cheese with them cows."

"Who owns the horses?" the young man asked.

"They was brung into town by a gambler that up and killed a man," the hostler explained. "He's in Sheriff Tate's jail right now. They are going to hang him in two days and the horses become property of the town. I have been asked to sell them."

"And if I was to buy one, you can assure me that I wouldn't be hung trying to ride it out of town?" Tom inquired.

Slapping his knee, the old hostler laughed until he coughed. "You sure ask some funny questions, sonny."

Tom had his eye on the tall bay. "When the town hangs the man, how much will they want for the one on the right?"

"My, oh my," the stoop-shouldered man exclaimed, "you do know how to pick the best one."

Ignoring the comment, Tom Franklin climbed between the poles and took a closer look at the bay. The horse's reddish-brown coat, still showing some winter hair, needed a brushing and the black mane and tail were a little tangled. "I can't agree with you, old man," Tom contradicted the hostler. "The animal needs a lot of cleaning up, and it'll need smithy work on the shoes. It's a gelding and can't be used for breeding, and the horse is awfully thin."

"Why hell, sonny," the hostler objected, "you don't want a fat and lazy horse. This here bay is built for work. Where you're looking to go, you won't need to be riding a show horse."

With skepticism in his voice, Tom asked, "What is the town asking for the animal?"

"Well, there I can help you," the old man said proudly. "The town council must have thought the animals was the only horseflesh west of the Mississippi with the prices they was talking about. I convinced them to sell the horses at a more reasonable price, so good folks like you could afford them."

"And that good price is?" the young man inquired.

"It sure as hell wasn't the $150 they was asking," the stoop-shouldered man responded. "I was able to get them down to $100."

"I assume you are talking about all four horses," Tom replied.

Again, the old man burst out laughing, "You are a funny one, sonny. I like you."

Then the old hostler moved close to the young man and talked softly, glancing around as he spoke, "You won't get them to budge from the price, and demand for horseflesh has doubled the cost in the last couple years. They don't know I got the gear that the horse came in with. The saddle is decent, and saddle bags for your belongings. They got to be worth $40. I can throw them in."

"I'll need a scabbard for the rifle," Tom reminded the man.

"Damn, you are being difficult, sonny," the hostler complained. "I'm already losing my profits on the gear."

The old hostler had managed to wear the young man down. Tom did like the bay and would need the rest of the gear for the horse. "Get it shoed and we have a deal," was his last offer.

"By God, I can do that myself," the hostler replied, with the look of joy on his old, wrinkled face.

"The name on the bill of sale will be Tom Franklin," he told the old man.

"Okay, sonny," the hostler said, "and you can call me, Billy." Then he asked, "You got a place to stay?"

"I'll be looking for one when I leave," Tom replied.

"It'll cost a dollar to board your new horse and you are welcome to sleep in the loft," Billy let the young man know.

To Tom's surprise, the hostler required the $101 on the spot and then led the bay to the livery as they headed back. Billy took the animal to the side, where he had a small smithy shop. He then returned, brought Tom to the tack room and pulled out a dusty saddle, some bags and reins. The young man knew that there was no way that this gear came in with the horses. It appeared to have been stored in the tack room for years.

Billy left him with the dusty gear, and headed over to shoe the horse. Tom saw a shelf with saddle soap and brushes. Having no place to go at the moment, he pulled the nail keg over and started working on the scarred, dusty leather.

It was early afternoon when Billy brought the bay back into the livery. Tom had finished working the leather on his new gear. To his surprise the saddle was in better shape than he had expected. A couple saddle strings needed to be replaced, and the cantle had a groove which appeared to have been caused by a bullet, but overall it would serve him well.

"I see you found the saddle soap," the hostler observed. "You done a fine job on the saddle and bags. I got some leather string you can have to replace the broken ones."

"I appreciate it," Tom told the man. "How long before I get the papers for the horse?"

Reaching into his leather apron, Billy pulled out a wrinkled slip and handed it to Tom. "Here you are, the bay is yours."

"Aren't we waiting for the hanging?" the surprised young man asked.

"No need," the hostler said. "Sheriff Tate ain't missed a hanging date yet. You can consider it a done deal." Handing the lead rope to Tom, he continued. "You want some oats for your horse? It's two bits."

Tom Franklin was taken off guard at how fast the bay went from being city property to his responsibility. "Give the horse a double portion, Billy."

"Put it in the stall next to the mule," the hostler instructed. "Then come into the smithy. I got coffee and beans heating on the forge."

Tom watched the hostler walk away. *He sure is a strange old man,* he thought.

After the weak coffee and slightly fermented beans, Tom returned to brush the bay. Billy had suggested he visit Jacob and Samuel Hawken's gun shop. It was frequented by hunters and trappers. They should know of anyone looking to add a man before heading west.

The young man took his new horse out for a ride, west of St. Louis. The bay responded well to slight commands and had a comfortable gait. Tom carried the Kentucky long rifle across the front of his saddle in case he saw some game, or someone who didn't look quite right.

Shortly before sunset, he returned to the livery with two rabbits hanging from the saddle horn. Billy was thrilled with the prospect of fresh meat and hurried to fire up the forge. There was a saloon just up the dusty street from the livery. While the hostler prepared the rabbit, Tom went to get them a bottle of rye.

Tom hadn't tended to frequent the drinking establishments back in Vermont. His folks had frowned on such things. During the trip west, he had taken a liking to the occasional drink. As he approached the saloon, the doors burst open in front of him, causing Tom to jump out of the way. A stocky dock worker came tumbling out of the saloon, followed by a big bruiser.

Several men followed the fight outside and were shouting encouragement to their favorites. Tom learned that the big bruiser was named Bart. Bart made short work of the dock worker and left the area staggering after more than enough to drink.

Following the crowd back into the saloon, Tom passed some broken chairs and a collapsed table. The patrons went back to having a good time, quickly forgetting about the fight. Pushing his way to the bar, he ordered a bottle of rye.

Looking around the room, he saw a mixture of trappers, buffalo hunters, and dock workers. It was a rough and tumble establishment. He felt a bit of excitement. These were the types of men he would be working and living with. Tom paid for the bottle, having one drink before heading back for his supper at the livery.

While eating the rabbit, which had been done quite nicely by the hostler, Tom told him about the fight. Billy shook his head. "The bars can be quite rough near the waterfront. They ain't nothing like what I hear the rendezvous is. Them western mountain men really know how to have a good time."

Wiping the meat juice from his whiskered chin, Tom asked, "It's kind of you to roast these rabbits, but ain't your wife expecting you at home?"

Grinning like the cat that caught the canary, Billy told him, "Tonight's her church social and I told her I had to get your horse ready for travel come morning and would have to work late."

Rain had started the during the night and there was still a cold drizzle falling when Tom climbed down from the loft. Sometime during the night, some others had joined him, no doubt staggering from the saloon to the livery.

The street was already busy in front of the livery, churning the dusty street to mud. Tom had talked for hours with Billy while they worked their way through the bottle. For a man who had never been out west, the hostler had a wealth of knowledge of life on the frontier.

Billy had the fire going in the potbelly stove near his office. The coffee was on, and he had slices of thick bread and butter sent by his wife, Esther. Tom sat eating while he watched the rain through the open front doors. While lying in the loft the night before, he had decided that he would check around St. Louis to find out if anyone heading west was looking for a man. If he found none, he would ride 10 – 12 days west to Independence and wait there for a caravan heading west.

After carefully packing his things into the saddlebags, and the larger items rolled up in his blanket roll, Tom prepared to leave. His ground tarp protected the blankets and he would wear his slicker. Billy suggested he spend a few days in St. Louis until he found some trappers. In June he could hire on to one of the caravans carrying items to the rendezvous.

Impatient to start west, Tom thanked the hostler for his hospitality and made the mercantile his first stop. He had a list of staples he would need for the trip to Independence. He stepped into the mercantile to the smells of leather goods, rope, oils, spices, and the coffee bubbling on the stove. An elderly man, who was balding and wearing spectacles, came out from the back.

"What can I help you with?" the merchant asked, noticing water dripping off Tom's slicker. Handing him his list, the young man browsed through the shelves of canned goods and household items. One shelf contained small boxes and bottles that promised to heal most anything that could ail a person.

Shortly, Tom left with a burlap bag containing his purchases. He draped his slicker over the bag as he rode up the muddy street towards the Hawkens' shop. He missed seeing Oli slogging along in the soupy street with his head down in his sodden clothes. Tom pulled his flat-brimmed hat down to keep the rain off his face.

The drizzle had stopped when Tom rode up to the Hawkens' shop. The long building had a front room with completed rifles, while most of the manufacturing was done toward the back. Three men were in the front room discussing rifles with customers. They all wore leather aprons and no doubt worked the machines or did assembly when there were no customers.

One of the men was just cashing out a customer. As the buckskin-clad customer left admiring his new rifle, the clerl turned to Tom, noting the Kentucky Long Rifle he was carrying.

Smiling, the man looked over the glasses that had slid down his nose. "You looking to have it converted to percussion or are you interested in replacing the rifle?"

"I'm here to trade this and get a Hawken .50," Tom replied.

Each of the rifles on display were handmade and most of them to order. The wait for a new rifle could be three weeks to a month. A few of them had been swapped for newer models, then re-worked and converted to percussion.

Tom decided that he would have to purchase one of the reconditioned rifles. He was given $10 credit for the long rifle and paid an additional $30 for the .50 caliber Hawken with caps, a mold, some powder, lead, and a small sack of pre-cast balls. The new Hawken was rifled to improve accuracy. The ten-pound rifle was shorter than the Kentucky rifle. For another $5 the man supplied a scabbard for Tom's saddle.

The young man stood staring at his new rifle with a smile as broad as that of a kid with a jar of peppermint sticks. "You got a good rifle there," a voice behind him said, startling Tom.

Turning, he looked into the gray eyes of a stocky man, around 40 years-old. The man extended his hand, "I'm Gus Whitestone." Gesturing over his shoulder, he added, "That's my brother, Hector." Gus and Hector Whitestone were at the gunsmith shop making a deal on a .53 caliber rifle. Tom noticed that Gus carried himself with an air of authority. He had a disheveled crop of dirty-blond hair and a wide moustache.

"Thank you," the proud new owner of the rifle replied. "I'm going to use it in the Rockies."

"You plan to be a mountain man," Gus surmised.

"That is my plan," Tom told him. "My brother and I came from Vermont to hunt buffalo or trap in the mountains." A cloud passed over the young man's face as he continued. "My brother was lost on the Ohio. Now I'm doing it for the both of us."

"Well, it's kind of early in the year to start trapping beaver," Gus replied. "I had a skinner that decided to go east and see his family. Me and Hector are looking for a man to come on our next buffalo hunt."

Unsure, Tom said, "I was hoping of doing some shooting with this here rifle. I've done some skinning in my days, but it's the shooting I'm looking forward to doing."

Gus had a hardy laugh. Still smiling, he told the young man, "If you can use the Hawken there, you'll get all the shooting you want."

Agreeing to go with the brothers, Gus then advised that Tom purchase a cap-and-ball side arm and an extra powder horn. The Hawken was a one-shot muzzle loader. In a firefight the six-shot Colt could mean the difference between life and death. Tom soon realized that of the two brothers, Gus was in charge.

The young man left St. Louis with the Whitestone brothers on a new adventure. He was heading out onto the open plains to become a buffalo hunter. Tom rode his long-legged bay. The scabbard held the new Hawken rifle. On his right hip was the Colt revolver and on the left a skinning knife.

His pants and shirt were wool, and his coat was buckskin with fringed sleeves. Tom's hat was dark leather, with a flat brim and round top. He wore low-heeled, high-top boots with his pants tucked in.

Tom blended well with the Whitestones. Their dress was similar to Tom's, except they wore lower-cut boots. The brothers drove a sturdy freight wagon pulled by four horses. A mule they called Ralph was tied to the back loaded with packs that didn't fit in the wagon. It would be used in the hunting grounds to move the downed buffalo. It would then haul the hides back to camp on a wooden sledge that was now in the wagon.

The rolling plains were covered with spring flowers. New grass was pushing through the dead, brown stems of the past year. Gus followed the muddy ruts of previous wagons that had headed for Independence, Missouri. They stopped near a stream to water the animals and eat a quick midday meal.

Hector wanted coffee and broke up some dry branches for a cook fire. "Hey, Tom," Gus called. "See the pronghorn on the side hill? Let's see how that new rifle works. I could go for some steaks for supper."

Pulling the Hawken from the scabbard, Tom's heart beat with excitement. He had shot the rifle a couple of times at the shop, but now he had the chance to show the Whitestones that he could be their man shooting buffalo.

Tom leaned it against the wagon. Taking what was needed from his possible bag, the young man loaded the Hawken. Seating the ball firmly into the barrel, Tom put the ramrod back under the barrel. He stepped into the open before placing the percussion cap on the nipple.

The young man had been loading and shooting muzzle loaders since he was 12, but with Gus watching him he felt like a greenhorn, fearful that the man wouldn't like something he did. Taking his time aiming, Tom pulled the set trigger. Then, lining up the blade sights, he touched off the front trigger. The rifle jumped in his hands as it sent the killing ball at the pronghorn.

The one he had shot at spun sprawling among the yellow and blue flowers. A second later the rest of the pronghorn bounded over the rise to safety. "I got it!" Tom shouted.

"That you did," Gus agreed. "Now go get the bugger."

Tom quickly gutted the animal before laying it across the back of the saddle and riding back to the wagon. His shot had been right behind the front shoulder, just where he had been aiming. He wanted to point this out to Gus, but thought better of it. The buffalo hunter would have expected him to aim there.

Hector had the coffee ready when he got back. Tom tossed the pronghorn into the wagon. They made a meal of hard bread and the coffee. Having eaten, the fire was doused, and Gus climbed onto the wagon. Looking down at the young man, he said, "That was good shooting."

Pleased with Gus' approval, Tom led the way along the rutted trail. The party continued until early evening. Gus pulled the wagon off the trail near a grove of cottonwood. Tom helped take care of the animals before skinning the pronghorn. It was much smaller than the deer he had hunted in Vermont. The three of them would eat most of it in one meal.

While Hector broiled the meat over the fire, Tom helped Gus rig the fly tarp. It was large enough for the three of them to sleep under. Their gear was placed under the wagon. The rain from the day before was gone, but clouds remained.

Grunting as he pulled the guy rope tight, Gus said, "We don't usually rig the tarp when traveling unless there's a chance of rain."

A constant breeze fluttered the canvas as the men devoured the juicy meat. Tom knew this scene would be repeated many times in the coming weeks. He looked at his traveling companions. The Whitestones would be good men to hunt with. Tom also believed he would learn much about living on the plains from Gus.

It took them three weeks to travel from St. Louis to the area Gus wanted to hunt. They were in the rolling hills above the Kaw River. Several times on the way they had passed small herds of buffalo and Tom wondered why Gus didn't stop and shoot some.

Finally, they stopped near a wide stream. That day they had passed large herds of grazing buffalo.

"Tomorrow is Sunday and we rest," Gus announced. "Come Monday, we start hunting."

Disappointed that they couldn't start shooting buffalo right off, Tom helped Hector set up camp while Gus tended to the team. "I could shoot a half-dozen buffalo and have them skinned before dark," the young man complained.

"Just be patient," Hector replied. "Soon you'll be looking forward to time off."

Tom was looking forward to the first day of shooting. He hardly slept that Sunday night. He was up before daylight and sat near the fire with his new Hawken cleaned and ready, cradled in his arms. Gus came back from relieving himself. "I hope I see the same enthusiasm every morning of the hunt."

The young man was determined not to disappoint Gus. He had always loved hunting and looked forward to watching the massive animals fall. The biggest thing Tom had shot in the past had been a bear that was getting into the apples on the farm in Vermont. It had weighed about 250 pounds and he had let it hang for two days near the road. He had been the hero of the neighborhood.

The day's hunt began with Tom riding his bay while Gus and Hector rode two of the team horses. Ralph followed them, dragging an empty sledge.

Tom asked Gus why they didn't use the horses for working in the hunting grounds.

"The horses could do the work of the mule," Gus replied, "but there ain't anything better than a noisy mule to warn you of any Indians sneaking up."

"So, it will be kept close to us at all times?" Tom asked.

"Yup."

That was some comfort to Tom. He had not seriously considered Indians out on the plains. The young man learned that he and Gus would be shooting while Hector loaded the rifles. Gus bought some newspaper and pillow ticking before leaving St. Louis. The paper was torn into squares. The measured gun powder was wrapped in these packets. The ticking was cut into pieces and saturated with grease, to use as patches.

Hector would tear the end off of a packet, then pour the powder into the rifle barrel. He would then place a greased patch over the end of the bore before ramming a ball down the barrel. This way, loading was faster and Hector didn't have to measure each load from the powder horn.

Gus told Tom that the buffalo didn't recognize gunshots as danger and would continue grazing as members of the herd were shot. Gus told him to pick smaller buffalo and leave the big bulls. The large hides were less valuable. He cautioned him about wounding an animal. It could start the rest running, so well-placed shots were important.

"Today we will shoot about a dozen buffalo," Gus said. "It will give us a chance to get some of the kinks out."

While he hadn't said anything about it, the young man knew that Gus wanted to give him a chance to learn about harvesting hides. Tom didn't care, as long as he got a chance to do some shooting. The young man was surprised at how close they got to the buffalo before setting up for shooting. Sitting impatiently, he watched as Gus shot seven of the wooly beasts.

Gus would take his time choosing an animal and then, after taking careful aim, he'd fire. For a moment, nothing would happen. Then one of the buffalo would go to its knees and slowly roll over onto its side. At most that animal would kick a few times, which was less than a buffalo rolling on its back dusting itself.

Finally, he waved Tom over. "Now it's your turn." There was one buffalo standing away from the others. That was the one Gus directed him to shoot. The young man's heart was pounding as he double checked his rifle. Then he took aim while pulling the rear trigger. Now the front hair trigger was set.

Tom squeezed the front trigger and the .50 caliber recoiled against his shoulder as smoke and fire burst from the barrel. The young man's eyes were fixed on the buffalo as he whispered a prayer that it would fall. Relief washed over him as he saw the buffalo sink to the ground.

After that Gus and Tom took turns shooting until 12 buffalo lay dead on the plain grass. Hector gathered up the loading material and put them into the shooting bag. "Let's get down there and skin the buggers before the wolves find them," Gus told the young man.

For a moment Tom stared, smiling at the buffalo they'd shot. He thought of all the people that meat would feed in Vermont. Then he hurried to get his bay and followed the sledge down to the kills. The young man dismounted near the first buffalo he had shot. He placed his hand on the massive shoulder. His eyes shining, he thought, *This one has to weigh over a thousand pounds.*

"We ain't here to admire them," Gus shouted. "Get the knife out and start skinning!"

Gus skinned two in the time it took Tom to do the one he had shot. As he skinned, he tried to take care not to damage the hide or get dirt on the carcass. That was when it sunk in, that they did not have to take care skinning. All they were after was the hide. The meat would be left.

Not wanting to disappoint Gus, the young man worked feverishly on the next four buffalo. Gus skinned the other five, seemingly without much effort. Hector would grab the hides from them and get them onto the sledge. Once he had all twelve loaded, he hauled them up to the wagon area to flesh and spread them out on the grass to dry. He tossed salt onto them to prevent rotting.

Gus had cut the tongue out of the first buffalo Tom had shot and some additional meat from the tenderloins. Holding them up he said, "We eat good tonight."

The young man climbed onto the bay, his clothes covered with blood and fat, and his arms aching with fatigue. In just a few hours, they had shot and skinned 12 buffalo. Gus had talked of trying to shoot 20 a day.

CHAPTER TWO

Tom Franklin leaned his head against the side of a Guernsey cow. He was stripping the milk into a wooden bucket. The rich, creamy liquid was covered by a layer of foam.

His mother was singing softly in the barnyard while feeding the chickens. He knew she would be wearing a gingham dress covered by a crisply-ironed apron.

He picked the bucket from under the cow. Careful not to spill any milk he was carrying, he hung the three-legged stool on the wall bracket. Ducking his six-foot frame under the low door of the barn, he headed across the yard to put the milk into the well to cool.

Isaac Franklin was trotting toward Tom, waving. Tom could see that his brother was saying something to him, but all he could hear was the braying of a mule. It looked like the sound was coming from Isaac!

Tom awoke suddenly. He had been dreaming. Realization came quickly. He lay in his blankets on the muddy ground, under the fly-tarp. The noise came from Ralph. One of the buffalo hunters was trying to put harnesses on him.

It was August 1839. Tom lay for a few more minutes under the tarp, enjoying the warmth of his blanket. For the past several weeks, shooting and skinning had become a blur. Tom had fallen into the daily routine. He would wake at sunrise to the cool, misty morning. Once the fire was started, the horses and mule needed tending. Breakfast was fried side meat, buffalo, or biscuits. Good, strong coffee helped the men wake up. The biscuits were made in the Dutch oven by Hector. The results were tough and slightly burned. Soaking them in coffee made the biscuits edible.

On a good day, the men would kill up to 25 buffalo. There were days that a good-sized group couldn't be found and they got fewer kills. Once the animals were downed, the rest of the day was spent skinning and processing the hides.

The smell of rotting carcasses was everywhere. The hides were equally foul-smelling. There was the constant buzz of flies. Crows, buzzards, wolves, and other carnivorous animals could be seen moving boldly around, feeding on the remains.

Mud, blood, and fat covered their clothes and equipment. Skinning the large beasts was all bull work. Hector had some iron stakes that could be driven through the nose of the buffalo to secure the animal. After a few slits were made, the mule was then tied to the hide so it could be stripped from the carcass. It made the skinning much faster.

At the end of the day, the last of the hides were loaded onto the sledge and Ralph would haul them back to the main camp. After folding and stowing the dry hides, the new ones were fleshed and spread for drying. The men would then clean up as best they could. Supper would be beans and buffalo tongue, or steaks taken from the more tender parts of the animals. These were broiled over a buffalo chip fire.

After a few stiff drinks of rye while readying their rifles and powder packets for the next day, the men turned into an exhausted sleep. They slept, depending on Ralph to alert them to intruders.

Gus had chosen to hunt near the western part of the Kaw River because the buffalo were plentiful, and it was seldom that they did not get their quota of 15 to 20 kills. They had to move often to get away from the rotting carcasses and follow the grazing buffalo. Gus and Hector did not believe in working on Sunday. When it rained, and during moves, hunting time was lost. Tom now welcomed the days off to rest and attempt to clean up.

There were several tribes competing for the buffalo. Occasionally, they would find the results of their kills. Tom didn't think it was right to take the hides and leave the meat to rot. But it was the nature of the business.

The Indians would use the animal, including many of the bones. The braves would bring down the beasts and their women would process the buffalo, drying the meat, saving the tallow, and tanning the hides. The bones were used for making tools, or broken to remove the marrow.

The Whitestones and Tom were intruding on their ancient hunting grounds. There was the constant fear of an attack. The hides were worth $3 each. In a six-week hunting trip, they could harvest over 300 hides. Each man would end up with $250 dollars after expenses. Most other jobs would provide $45 for the same amount of time.

It was risk and reward, the way they saw things. There were other buffalo hunters on the plains, but due to the vast area other men were seldom seen.

One Sunday, Gus told Tom that there was stream five miles southwest of them. He had been able to see groves of cottonwood along it from a rise. Tom decided that it was a good opportunity to get a proper bath and maybe some fish for supper. And, most of all, he would get away from the smell of the hide wagon.

Against Hector's better judgment, Tom saddled the bay and headed west. The August sun was warm. The rolling plains were spotted with the purples, yellows and reds of the wild flowers. He could see herds of buffalo as he rode and made notes for tomorrow's hunt.

The stream ran into the Kaw River as it wound through the plains. Tom sat under a large cottonwood with his fishing line in a slowly-moving pool on a bend. Next to Tom lay four plump trout. He had a small wood fire burning with three more fish broiling.

Tom thought about the times he and his brother would fish in the creek next to the farm in Vermont. Isaac had been a good fisherman and had the touch to catch the wily bass. He would have loved the ease of catching these trout.

While Tom was enjoying the change from buffalo to trout for his midday meal, he heard shooting to the south. *Hunting on Sunday, you will have bad luck the rest of the week,* Tom thought.

His clothes and body were scrubbed clean with a soft soap Gus had made from buffalo tallow and wood ashes. Tom napped while his clothes dried.

It was early afternoon when Tom swung his lanky frame into the saddle. It felt great to be clean. A stringer of trout hung on his saddle. He looked to the south. It had been some time since they'd gotten any news from other hunters. The shots he'd heard couldn't have been more than a mile away.

Turning his horse south, he set out to visit the men. They should just about be finished with skinning the animals. He had extra fish and decided he would share some with them.

Tom saw smoke on the horizon. He was glad that their camp was close. Tom trotted the bay in the direction of their fire. Riding over the rise, he stopped his horse in shock!

Before Tom lay the bodies of four men, stripped and mutilated. Their heads were covered with blood from being scalped. The empty hide wagon was the source of the smoke Tom had seen. It had been burned and was still smoldering.

Any horses were gone except for one that had been killed during the skirmish. Any guns and powder were gone. Tom urged his horse toward the carnage. He looked around with the feeling that eyes were on him and arrows would soon follow. He dismounted near the wagon. Tom tried to make his six-foot frame small. The hunters' supplies were spread around the ground. A bag of flour emptied out onto the green grass caught Tom's attention. For a moment he thought, *What a waste.*

His eyes went back to the dead men, and he felt ashamed for the thought. Tom knew that smarter men than him would know what to do now. Should he bury the men, or should he run? Visions of the wild animals and birds feeding on the buffalo carcasses came to mind. He knew that he couldn't leave them like this.

There was a short-handled shovel in the ransacked gear near the wagon. Tom began to dig, keeping the mutilated bodies behind him. As he dug into the unyielding dirt, sweat stung his eyes, causing tears to run down his cheeks. The truth was, the tears were caused as much by the emotions he felt as the sweat.

Tom's clean clothes were stained with dirt and sweat as he kept drying his hands while digging the graves. He wished that the holes were deeper, but frayed nerves would not let him take the time. It was two hours from sunset when the men were buried. He paused to say a few words over them.

Once in the saddle, Tom felt high and exposed. He kept the bay in the dips as much as possible. He could not get the sight of the scalped men's unseeing eyes and slashed bodies out of his mind. He had wrapped them in blankets spared from the fire before dragging them to the graves. Tom urged the bay to a trot, then into a gallop. He was happy to be away from the massacre.

Gus and Hector stood looking his way as he galloped the lathered horse. He slowed the exhausted animal to a walk and continued to the camp. Both of the Whitestones had their rifles cradled in their arms. Tom slid off the bay and leaned on the horse, his legs shaking. While gasping for breath, he told Gus and Hector what he had found. Gus kicked at a clod of dirt and looked at the horizon.

"Damn!" he exclaimed. Gus turned back to Tom. "You best walk that horse a bit more and then rub him down good."

Not even the trout raised the mood that night. Every sound in the dark made the men jump. Ralph calmly pulled at the wild grass, unconcerned with the normal nightlife. "How many Indians were there?" Gus inquired.

"I don't know, Gus. I was so scared that all I could think of was burying them and getting away from there."

Hector stared at the fire. "I don't believe I could have stayed and buried them."

Tom moved away from the fire with a cup of coffee. "It's not good to stare into the fire, Hector. I believe you would have buried them. Once you saw them lying there, you couldn't ride away."

"Do you know what kind they were?" Gus asked.

"I'm not sure, Gus," Tom replied. "There weren't any arrows left behind. Not that it would have helped. I guess the hides were packed on the horses and hauled away. Their food stuff was spread around. I did find an old receipt in a discarded shirt for hides they had sold. It was made out to Charlie Moss."

"I imagine most of the sign was trampled by their unshod ponies," Hector figured.

Tom felt a cold realization sweep over him. "The horses were shod."

Not comprehending what Tom had said, Gus continued. "I am surprised they wouldn't take the food. Store-bought grub is hard to come by, and seldom left behind. A brave could be a hero to his squaw bringing something like that in."

"Gus, Gus, did you hear what I said?" Tom repeated. "The horses had shoes."

The men stared at each other. It sunk in that there was something wrong with what Tom had found. While the Indians might be riding stolen horses with shoes, most did not because they required reworking every four to six weeks. Hector was a good farrier and took care of their animals. In this attack, there should have been some unshod tracks.

Scratching his head, Gus looked at Tom. "We got to go back in the morning and take another look."

CHAPTER THREE

The men decided to break camp. It was time to move and look for better hunting. There were over 125 hides on the wagon, the reward from 18 days of actual hunting. Hunting time had been lost during the trip across the plains from St. Louis. And then there were moving days and Sundays. Still, they were happy with the results so far.

Tom led the way to the site of the attack. It was as he had left it. Four fresh mounds of dirt marked the location of the graves. Gus stopped them several paces from the burned wagon.

Climbing down from their wagon, Gus circled the camp and looked for sign. Tom and Hector watched as he stopped and squatted down, then stood and moved to another area. Slowly, he made his way around and back to the wagon.

Walking back to their wagon, Gus leaned against the wheel and stared at the graves. "The men were scalped, stripped, and mutilated?"

"Yes, they were," Tom replied.

"Well, we got us some bad men out here," Gus sighed, "but they weren't Indians."

What Gus had found were six sets of shod horses coming into the camp. Three were ridden and three were being led. The horses had been tied to the burned wagon at one time. Puddles of blood on the grass showed where the four men had fallen. The bodies were then dragged a bit and mutilated.

The burned wagon tracks were deep coming to the camp. There were signs of lots of activity around it. The area was muddy and well-trod, just like the area around their hide wagon before a move. It had been loaded with hides.

The dead men's mid-day dishes were next to the fire and a half-empty coffee pot was left. A pot of beans was tipped, spilling onto the prairie grass.

Gus began to speak, as much to himself as to Hector and Tom. "Charlie Moss and his men had just set down to a Sunday meal. Three riders came up leading pack horses. No doubt they were invited to join and eat. The hunters were shot and then dragged away from the fire."

"The hides were most likely transferred to the pack horses. After eating the dead men's meal, they made the killings look like an Indian attack. When they left, it was to the northwest. Their pack horses were making deeper tracks."

Tom stared at Gus with his mouth hanging open. "What kind of men would do that?"

"There are many lawless men out here looking for opportunities to make easy money. It is simple to make it look like others done it," Gus said, shaking his head.

Hector sat on the wagon staring at the four mounds, his jaw clenched tight.

Gus took Tom around the camp, pointing out the sign he had seen. He also pointed to some horse tracks with identifying marks.

"If you take your time, you can pretty much put the story together of what happened," Gus told Tom, "and you will notice that each man and horse has unique characteristics in their tracks. Later, if you come across them again, you will know it is the same man or horse."

Tom walked around the camp, trying to put the story together like Gus had told it. Much of what he said Tom could see. But Tom realized that if he hadn't been told what to look for, it was doubtful he would have recognized the significance of most of the sign.

He appreciated the importance of what Gus was showing him, and he made a promise to spend more time seeing what was around him, rather than just looking.

Walking back to their wagon Tom said, "I saw some decent size bunches of buffalo yesterday. Maybe we should head that way and make camp."

Gus placed his hand on Tom's shoulder. "We got other work to do. By the direction these killers took, they're headed for a trading post near where the Kaw and the Missouri Rivers meet. It's about five days from here."

Resting his hand on his Colt, Gus looked in the direction the killers had gone. "We got to bring justice to the men they killed."

Tom did not understand what Gus was talking about. That was the work of a sheriff or marshal. The three of them were just hunters.

Before leaving the burned-out wagon, Gus carved some words in the side.

C Moss and men kilt by white men August 1839

"We don't want others coming onto the site and jumping to the wrong conclusion," Gus stated. "Indians do enough on their own without having to be blamed for another's bad deeds."

With Gus and Hector up on the wagon and Ralph tied to the back, the group headed northwest, following the tracks. Tom glanced back at the burned-out wagon. He caught a glimpse of movement.

Stopping the bay, he turned to look. There was nothing there. "Maybe one of the men's ghosts," he thought. A shiver went through him.

It was mid-afternoon when the three came up on a buffalo wallow. Hector noticed a bundle sticking out from under the edge. It was items from the murdered men. A quick examination revealed an empty money belt with 'C Moss' engraved in it. There was a letter to Charlie from a sister in Boston, Massachusetts. Gus carefully put it into his pack.

"We'll send her a letter about her brother, first chance we get."

Tom stared at Gus. He had become a different man since the killings. His easy smile had disappeared, and his eyes were cold and determined. The way he looked for details made Tom think he had done this kind of work before.

Each time they reached a place where the killers had camped, Gus would stop short and spend time looking the area over. Once, he found some feminine articles that had been discarded. No doubt it was booty from another ambush.

Tom kept seeing the movement behind them. He was never able to make it out. Gus had noticed it and told him it was some kind of animal. Maybe a wolf or coyote tracking them.

Two days out of the trading post, Tom sat staring out into the plains after supper. The evening was cool and the warmth of the hot tin cup of coffee in his hands felt good. He caught movement out of the corner of his eye.

He continued to look straight out, hoping to catch another glimpse of the shadowy figure. He heard the breathing. Something was stalking him. Slowly, he lowered his hand to the Colt. He slipped the loop off the hammer and waited.

"Are you going to feed that mutt something?"

Tom's heart jumped in his throat at the sound of Gus' voice.

"Well, either shoot it or feed it. Lord knows, it has followed us for the last three days," Gus laughed.

Tom heard whining from outside the fire light. It was a dog. Probably the prior owner was one of the murdered men. Tom coaxed the animal closer to the fire with a piece of biscuit.

"That will teach it to come to our fire," Hector chuckled.

The dog was a brown and tan mix breed. It had an angry-looking wound on its rump that it had been doing its best to keep clean. It stayed out of reach and watched the men.

"Looks like our killers took a shot at the animal," Tom concluded.

The morning came with no sign of the dog. The biscuit still lay were Tom had left it. As they traveled toward the trading post, the dog was sighted once in a while following them from a distance.

The plains were starting to show more groves of trees. Several winding brooks were draining into the Kaw River. The killer's tracks were easy to follow. No attempt had been made to hide them. Once, a buffalo cow was found with the back loins cut out. The men had been too lazy to skin the animal and add the hide to their load.

Gus pointed out that the kill was less than a day old. Few flies were attacking the carcass. The men they followed were not far ahead.

As the trail led them closer to the trading post, converging tracks made it harder to identify their quarry. There was little doubt about their destination, so Gus was not worried about losing them.

The trading post was located near the Missouri River. There was the Westport Landing nearby. Here, the buffalo hides would be transported by steamboats to eastern cities by way of the Missouri and Mississippi Rivers.

The trading post was an impressive building. The log walls reached two stories. A second single-story building located 50 feet away was the warehouse to store the hides between steamboat trips.

There were shade trees in front of the trading post, and a long porch across the front with benches. A small wooden table with two wooden stools had a checkerboard waiting for players.

Tom watched as Gus looked the area over. There were several makeshift camps along the river bank, spreading up towards the east. Even with the killers somewhere around, Tom felt safe for the first time in a while with folks around.

"I saw a discarded whiskey bottle at their first camp," Gus said. "I figure they got it from the supplies of the men they killed. I didn't see any after that, so these boys will be thirsty. More than likely they headed straight away to sell the hides."

Tom and the Whitestones set up camp under some oak trees away from the river. The horses and mule were rubbed down and picketed on a thick patch of grass. Tom took some side meat and placed it near the trees.

The three brushed their clothes a bit and headed for the trading post. Tom noticed that Gus had the loop off his side arm. Tom ducked through the low door into the dim light of the building. A few moments were taken to let their eyes adjust.

The building was divided into two sections. One section was filled with the supplies of various types. The other half was a saloon with a sturdy plank bar on the back wall. The saloon was filled with the smell of unwashed bodies, seasoned buffalo hides, spilt rye, and stale beer.

There were two groups of men standing at the bar drinking. Three tables had men playing cards. A merry gentleman in a derby hat sat at the piano, doing his best to perform on the out of tune instrument.

Tom looked intently at the piano player. "I believe I know that man."

"Know who?" Hector asked.

"The piano player. I believe it is Jinx from the landing on the Ohio River." Tom smiled. It faded as he thought about his brother Isaac. Isaac had been killed a couple days before they reached that landing.

Gus chose a table near the door and took the chair next to the wall. The bartender called to them, "Beer or rye?"

"Rye, thank you, and bring the bottle," Hector called back.

The bartender came over with three glasses and a bottle of something he was passing off as rye.

"That'll be a dollar," the portly bartender said with a nasal tone. He had greasy black hair plastered to his scalp.

Dropping a coin onto the table, Gus looked up. "We've got some hides to sell."

Grabbing up the coin, the bartender looked the three over. "A boat will be here in the morning. Have the hides near the landing. If they ain't rotten, you'll get $2.50 each."

Gus held out his glass to let the bartender pour. "Has anyone else sold any hides the past day or so?"

"No sir, not when the boat is so close to coming. The boss don't want to handle them any more than he has to." Quickly, the bartender turned away and went back behind the bar.

The rye was weak, except for the taste of pepper. A dollar was a lot to spend for what they were drinking.

"That's them," Gus whispered, nodding at one of the groups at the bar.

Tom and Hector looked where Gus was motioning.

"How do you know?" Tom asked in a hushed voice.

"The man had his boot sole tipped up a second ago. It had a groove cut across it from a rock or something. That boot made some of the tracks we have been following."

He stared intently at Gus. Tom was expecting him to jump to his feet and start cutting loose with the handgun. Instead, Gus tossed down his drink and looked at Tom and Hector.

"Let's get us some supper."

Tom went over to Jinx and chatted for a moment. Jinx laughed as he played. He had left the Ohio River landing and had just gotten into the area on the last steamboat.

He recommended the men eat at a boarding house just north of the trading post. Tom promised to come back again and listen to his playing.

Jinx was right. The meal at the boarding house was better than average. Slabs of tender roast buffalo, tasty gravy, and some type of greens with bits of bacon cooked with it. There was also a large basket of flaky biscuits in the center of the table that could be used to sop up the gravy. Two short and stocky ladies bustled around the tables, making sure everyone had plenty to eat and keeping coffee mugs filled.

While Tom waited, Gus didn't say another word about the men he had spotted in the saloon. With supper done, the ladies treated everyone to a large piece of custard pie.

Gus had gotten some cigars while at the trading post. He now handed one to Tom and Hector. Soon they were casually walking back to their camp, enjoying the pungent flavor from the smokes.

Hector got the fire going and filled the coffee pot to heat. It had been dark about an hour. The lights from the buildings below sliced through the night. The out-of-tune music from the piano could be heard in the distance.

Tom saw that the side meat was gone from near the tree. He emptied the scraps from his bandana onto the ground next to the tree. Along with the meat scraps was half a biscuit.

"You'll probably draw skunks to our camp before you coax that dog," Gus teased.

Hector roasted coffee beans in the blackened frying pan and used a Parker coffee mill to grind them. Once the water was boiling, Hector added a portion of the coffee grounds, saving the rest for future pots. A dash of cold water was added to stop the foaming. Soon they were all sitting, enjoying hot black coffee and the cigars.

"What are you going to do?" Tom asked Gus.

"About what?" Gus replied.

Tom let out a heavy sigh.

"I know you have thought of nothing but the men since we saw them," Gus said. "Tonight was not the night to do anything. We had a good supper and some good cigars. They can't get rid of their hides any quicker than we can. Come morning, we will deal with them."

Tom was up before daylight. He pulled his boots on and strapped on his gun. While relieving himself, he noticed that the meat scraps and biscuit were gone. Smiling, he returned to roll up his bedroll.

He saw Hector was still sleeping, but Gus was gone. Gus' blankets were neatly folded and some sticks had been added to the coals on the fire and were now smoldering. Tom couldn't remember if the bed was empty when he first got up.

Hector and Tom were sitting at the fire, with side meat sizzling in the fry pan when Gus returned.

"Have some coffee, Gus?" Tom asked.

"I believe I will, thank you."

Blowing on his cup of coffee, Gus took a sip. "Their camp is about a quarter-mile upriver. They have nine horses. Six are probably theirs and the other three came from the hunters. It looks like they drank quite heavily last night. No doubt they're spending the money from Charlie Moss' money belt."

"They got three piles of hides, probably 100 in total. My guess is they were all from Charlie Moss and his men."

Gus reached into his pack and took out a short iron which looked like a mini branding iron. "This here I got from the burned-out wagon. I noticed some letters burned into the side of the wagon. Some men like to tag the inside of their hides with an iron like this. Helps to identify their hides from everyone else."

Gus set the iron to one side and picked up a tin plate to have breakfast. Hector had brought biscuits home from the boarding house. They tasted great dipped in the fried meat drippings.

With the morning meal done, and the dishes rubbed clean with sand, the men headed for the landing with their hides. The steamboat was impressive. The men drove their wagon down to the river and saw the colorful boat with tall, black stacks tied to the shore. Gray smoke from the boilers rose lazily into the morning sky. The captain hit the steam whistle a couple extra times to announce to all that it was time to bring their hides down.

A huge, red-faced man sat next to a rough plank counter supported by two barrels. He had four blacks with him who would move the hides after they were tallied. Money was counted quickly, and for a big man he had quick hands. No doubt each count went in his favor.

Gus drove the wagon up at his turn. Hector and Tom helped to unload the hides. The count was 143. They were paying $2.50 for late summer hides. The coat was thinner than the early spring hides, which could bring as much as $5.00 each.

Gus made sure the huge man counted out $357.50 to the penny. Each of them would end up with $100 after expenses. Gus kept track of expenses and put that money up for the venture.

Tom saw Gus chatting with the huge man for a bit after the sale. He showed him something from his coat, but Tom couldn't catch what it was.

Hector led the team and wagon to a clear spot away from the sales platform. Gus got his Hawken .53 and checked the loads in his revolver. Hector and Tom did the same.

They made themselves comfortable on some sacks of beans that had been unloaded from the steamboat. The sale of the hides was brisk. Two men from the trading post were moving about the customers with pails of beer. Another followed with a sack of tin mugs. Gus bought three mugs of beer for two cents each.

Gus noticed the men they'd followed leading their pack horses toward the landing. All three had unkempt beards and rabbit skin caps. Their buckskin breeches were stained, as well as the buckskin shirts. The men laughed and poked at each other as they led the horses.

"The huge fellow, Al Johnson, knew Charlie Moss," Gus informed them. "He is familiar with Charlie's marking. This is his town and he said he would take care of things. We are just here for backup."

The three buckskin-covered men dumped the hides from their pack horses next to the counter.

Glancing at the hides, Al asked without looking up, "Did Charlie come with you?"

The leader of the three scowled, "We don't know no Charlie."

Tom watched as a sawed-off double barrel scatter gun appeared from below the plank counter. "You got his hides. Where is Charlie?"

Tom could see the markings. A two-inch, square CM brand on the inside of the hides.

"What the hell are you talking about?" the leader blustered.

Four neatly-dressed men in dark wool trousers and dark wool coats stepped up behind the three men. Each had a single-shot pistol drawn.

Al Johnson stood up to his full six-foot plus height and announced to the crowd, "These three men have been identified as the murderers of Charlie Moss and his men. They have with them the hides from Charlie's wagon." The big man lifted a hide showing the CM brand.

"I therefore find them guilty of robbery and murder. Without further ado, they will be hung until dead."

Tom watched in wonder at the swift justice. There was a brief struggle as the three men were grabbed and their hands tied. The leader shouted obscenities at Al Johnson while the other two pleaded for their lives.

The three men were put onto the pack horses. The dark-coated men led the horses to a spreading live oak tree. Ropes were promptly tossed over a branch and the nooses fitted around the men's necks.

Tom saw that one of them had wet himself and urine was running out the bottom of his buckskin pants.

The three horses were slapped and before one could say, "May God have mercy on their souls," the men were kicking and struggling at the ends of the ropes.

Tom could have sworn that it took them longer to die than the trial took. That is, if it could be called a trial.

Gus saw the shock on Tom's face. "It is called frontier justice. There was no doubt the men were guilty of killing Charlie and his crew. Who knows how many others died at their hands? The plains will be a safer place with the likes of these gone."

Gus gave Al Johnson the letter from Charlie's sister. Al promised to have Charlie's share of the money from the sale of the hides sent to her. He also knew the other three men and would get their shares sent to their families.

"Will he actually do it?" Tom asked Gus.

"Well, Al Johnson will cheat you out of your change on a sale. But he is a man of his word. If he says the money will be sent, it will be sent."

Tom glanced back as they headed toward their camp. The sale of hides continued like nothing had happened. The three men now hung silently on the oak tree and not a hundred feet away, beer was being drunk and hides were being counted.

CHAPTER FOUR

Tom Franklin and the Whitestone brothers left the Westport landing heading northwest. They were feeling very good about their summer hunt. With each of them clearing $300, it felt like whatever they wanted was theirs to have. The wagon was loaded with supplies for the next hunt.

It was decided that the hunt would be in the high plains north of the Platte River. Hunters in Westport had talked of a moving sea of buffalo. With luck, they could harvest a wagon load of hides and go on to Fort William on the Laramie River and sell them.

The price per hide at Fort William was not as good as at Westport, but the taking of buffalo would be faster. Therefore, it would make the return as good.

The men knew that they were heading into Cheyenne and Lakota territory. Gus figured 40 buffalo a day was possible, especially when using a nose stake and the mule to skin the animals. The team of horses could also be used.

"Three weeks at most," Gus said confidently, "and we will be heading for Fort William with over 700 hides."

"How long will it take to get to Fort William?" Hector asked.

"Steady travel, I would say a couple weeks, depending how far west we go. With time for hunting, we will be in Fort William before the snow flies. We can winter there and then get in on an early spring hunt for some high-priced hides."

Gus had it all figured out, Tom thought. He wished that he could plan as well. Someday he would be on his own in the mountains trapping. Planning like Gus could make the winter of trapping profitable, not to mention it could save a man's life.

The plains grasses were starting to turn brown. The rains were less frequent and the wind blew every day. Dust devils would spring up, and if one hit them it was like being blasted with bird shot. Tumble weeds were breaking loose from their roots and rolling across the grasses, dropping seeds for next year's crop.

Tom continued to ride the bay, while Gus and Hector rode in the wagon. Ralph, with packs, obediently followed behind the wagon. Their new addition was the dog. It now trotted beside Tom, having finally adopted him.

The dry conditions made it necessary to follow the winding streams as they travelled north. Tom was half-dozing on the bay when he heard Gus shout, "Pull up near the willows and make camp!"

Surprised, Tom wondered why. It was only mid-afternoon. Then he saw the western horizon.

There was a brown cloud hugging the plain and heading in their direction. A dust storm was coming!

Without instruction, the men rushed to set up camp. The fly-tarp was secured to the west side of the wagon and staked to the ground. The animals were watered and tied to a picket line in the willows. Bags of supplies were pulled from the wagon and stacked to offer additional protection from the sides.

There was a pool of water in the slow-flowing stream and a rope was strung from the wagon to a willow sapling near it. It would become critical if the blinding sand storm lasted any length of time. The men had their gear and rifles stowed under the cramped quarters of the tarp. With their canteens filled and the crude refuge finished, the men sat and waited.

The dust storm slammed into their camp with a fury. Their shelter was quickly filled with blinding dust and the storm tried to tear it apart. The men had neckerchiefs over their noses, attempting to keep the dust out of their lungs.

Tom had pulled his wool blanket over his head and in the darkness he saw flashes of light from the static caused by the churning dust. It was difficult to tell day from night and the three men huddled under the tarp, the hours dragging on.

Hector had dug some biscuits from one of the packs. They were rapidly coated with dust and sand. The stale biscuits grated between their teeth from the sand. The last of them were finally discarded as being impossible to eat.

Hunkering under their blankets and chewing on jerky washed down with sips of water became the way of life for the moment. The men took turns going out and checking on the animals, sponging their noses to get out the sand. The horses and mules stood heads down with their rumps to the storm.

The dog started out lying under the wagon with its nose under its tail. After a bit, Tom felt it pushing against his blanket for protection. Tom lifted the edge so it could crawl under. Throughout the night and next day, the wind and sand continued. Gus worried about getting water to the animals. Even if they could move them to the stream, the water would be mixed with dust and sand.

Sometime during the second night, the wind died and the dust began to settle. Tom peered out from the edge of their shelter and was unable to see any stars. Attempts to breathe without the neckerchiefs caused the men to cough. Gus and Tom ventured out and led the animals to the pool, allowing them to drink. In the dark they were unable to see the water, but when the young man attempted to drink a handful, he had to spit it out due to the muddy taste and feel.

As they returned leading the animals, they caught the flicker of fire. Hector had stored some kindling in the shelter before the storm hit, and he had now lit it to attempt to make coffee. With the horses and mule tied to the picket line, the two men returned to the shelter. The small fire revealed evidence of the storm damage.

One corner of the tarp had come loose and ripped. The goods were covered with dust, every opening penetrated with the fine powder. While they had tried to protect their rifles and revolvers under the blankets, they would require tearing down to clean out the abrasive dust. What little water they had left in the canteens was poured into the pot and Hector made them coffee to drink while they waited for morning.

It took most of the next day to clean sand and dust out of their gear and supplies. Hector spent extra time trying to make a hearty meal of beans, side meat, and biscuits. Extra molasses was added to the beans and honey was brought out for the coffee and biscuits. While it was good to have a solid meal after a day and a half of jerky, the men could still feel the dusty grit in the food.

Their spirits rose when they could see several hundred buffalo from the camp. The animals shook and rolled, raising clouds of dust from their coats. Some of the young bulls bellowed and challenged the older bulls for possession of the breeding cows.

"Why aren't we shooting?" Hector asked.

"We are too far from Fort William," Gus told his brother. "Once we are on the other side of the Platte River, we start hunting."

Tom understood the burden of carrying the hides across hundreds of miles. If the buffalo were as thick as promised, once across the Platte it would take only few weeks to finish the hunt.

The wagon was packed and the horses hitched. It was time to continue west. Three days had been lost with the storm, not to mention the animals being weaker from lack of grazing. Despite everything, it felt great to be on the move.

The dog trotted alongside Tom, carrying a partially eaten rabbit. "Packing your supper, aren't you, dog?"

Two weeks later they were at the Platte River. Tom found a good spot to cross. A sandbar emerged halfway across the river. It became deeper after that, but it was a short swim to the other side.

Gus had sealed the boards in the wagon with pine tar to ensure it would float. Dripping and chilled by the late summer air, the men and horses made it to the other side. The dog had disappeared. Maybe the river had changed its mind about partnering with them.

A good camp was found close to a large herd of buffalo. A cold wind was blowing from the west. They were on the high plains. The days could be uncomfortably hot while the nights were bone-chilling cold.

The men woke to a bright orange sunrise. The dog had returned and was lying next to Tom. Hector was excited. Today they would hunt. The horses snorted in the morning air, sending out clouds of steam. The mule took a vicious kick at Gus while being readied and narrowly missed.

Tom couldn't believe it, but he was looking forward to buffalo tongue for supper. The men set up less than a quarter-mile from the camp and began shooting buffalo. The first day's hunt was everything they'd hoped for. Within an hour, 26 buffalo lay dead on the plain.

Realization of the work ahead of them sank in as the skinning started. They split into two skinning teams. Tom used the mule and skinned the smaller buffalo, while Gus with the team skinned the bigger animals. Hector hitched two horses to the wagon and followed them around, preparing and loading hides.

The sun had set before they skinned the last animal. Covered with sweat, blood, and fat they moved away from the carcasses and went back to the camp. Hector had gathered buffalo chips for their fire.

The camp was set up next to a small pool of water left over from a dried-up stream. The thirsty animals had it trampled to mud before the men had a chance to wash. Tom tried to wipe the blood and fat off his hands and arms on the brown grass. Coffee, jerky, and day-old biscuits made up their meal. Exhausted, the men ate slowly, without conversation.

The night was cold and clear, with a star-studded sky. Tom felt like he could reach up and pluck a star out of the heavens. He felt mighty small on the wide-open plain. With every muscle aching, Tom vowed that they would shoot fewer buffalo tomorrow.

The morning sky was gray, with low clouds, when they woke up. The air smelled damp, but it was not raining. Tom opened his eyes. Stiffly, he sat up and rubbed his face. The familiar smell of buffalo hides was back.

All three were slow getting to the fire for breakfast. Hector seemed least affected by the long day of harvesting hides.

"Today, I think I will leave the wagons somewhere in the middle and have camp set up. I can then use the horses and sledge to haul the hides back. That way at the end of the day . . ." Hector's voice trailed off.

He was staring toward the bloody carcasses out on the plain. Gus and Tom looked over and froze. There were a half a dozen Cheyenne braves sitting among the skinned buffalo, watching the camp.

The men's rifles were in the wagon, leaning against the seat, cleaned and ready for the days shooting. Only Gus was wearing his handgun. The others were hanging off the tailgate of the wagon.

"Boys, let's take up our coffee and walk casually back to the wagon," Gus said. "If they move in our direction, we will get our rifles."

"They aren't loaded, Gus," Tom reminded him.

The braves started to slowly ride through the dead buffalo, staying parallel to the men.

"They won't know the rifles are empty," Gus said. "Right now, they are looking at a lot of buffalo we killed yesterday with the rifles. They will figure we have strong medicine and may decide to stay out of range."

The mule caught scent of the Cheyenne and began to bray. The dog lay next to Tom's feet and growled softly.

The braves suddenly broke out into a series of shrill cries and, waving their weapons in the air, rode away over the rise.

Tom took a sip of his coffee. He noticed that his hand was shaking and the coffee was cold. He looked at Gus. His face was still and his eyes determined as he loaded his .53 caliber. He handed Hector the other rifle to load.

Tom strapped on his Colt and checked the loads. Then, retrieving his Hawken, he loaded it.

Tom remembered a time he and Isaac had tried to empty a pond near the farm to get at the fish. After an hour scooping with a bucket, they'd given it up as an impossible task.

Now, looking at the three single-shot rifles and the number of possible Cheyenne out on the plain, he got the same hopeless feeling.

"Hey, you two," Gus scolded, "they don't want to die any more than we do. Odds are the Cheyenne might figure we are too strong to attack."

"I knew they would be out here," Hector said with a quivering voice, "but I didn't think we would see them."

"If you don't see them, you best start worrying. The Cheyenne saw all the dead buffalo that were not there the day before. What we saw were some impressed braves surveying our work," Gus said firmly. He then started hitching the horses for the day's work.

A little caution was in order. The wagon was left near a buffalo wallow. Extra water was put into the wagon. Extra caps, powder, and bullets were cached in the wallow.

The shooting stopped after 21 buffalo were downed. The men had gotten a later start and wanted to be back in camp before dark.

Tension was as thick as molasses as they skinned the animals. The men were depending on Ralph or the dog to warn them if the Cheyenne came back. The cloud cover stayed, which helped with the heat.

Tom and Gus kept their revolvers hanging on the mule and horses. It would prevent the actions from getting full of blood and fat. The rifles were also in scabbards on their animals. Hector wore his handgun. His rifle was loaded and left near the wagon.

During a short noon break, Tom was touching up his blade on a stone when he heard the dog growl a warning. He looked in the same direction as the dog. Slowly, he made out the dark top of several heads watching them from just beyond a rise.

His throat was dry and he found it hard to swallow. He reached for his canteen. Again, his hand was shaking. He cleared his throat and nodded for Gus to look.

"I see them. I have been catching movement for the past two hours," Gus breathed. "It don't make sense what they're doing."

"Maybe they're evaluating our firepower," Tom suggested.

"After one round of shooting this morning, they knew our firepower."

"I can't eat, let's get these beasts skinned," Tom said.

It was almost sunset when the last hides were spread to dry near the wagon. The men built a small fire on the bank of the wallow. Their horses and mule were watered and rubbed down. The animals were kept close in, with marginal grass to eat.

Hector had supper ready. The beans could have used a bit more time on the fire and the biscuits were a little doughy. It was late and the men didn't want to let them cook longer.

Tom was surprised at how good the meal tasted. The doughy rolls were easier to chew and the crunchy beans were a nice change. He said as much to Hector.

"I appreciate your kind words. I can't even eat tonight," Hector admitted.

The fire was allowed to burn down as darkness engulfed the men. They didn't bother to make up the bedrolls. It was doubtful anyone would sleep tonight. Gus sat on the edge of the wallow, looking out into the dark plains.

Tom dozed off and on during the long night. The dog would growl softly and alert him. Soon his eyes would get heavy again. The mule stood quietly in the dark. He could hear the even breathing of Hector. He smiled in the dark. "Some guys can sleep through anything."

Gus was still sitting on the edge of the wallow when the eastern sky began to get light. Tom didn't know if he had slept or not. He knew Gus hadn't moved much.

Tom saw the dog lying on its side, sleeping. With that vote of safety, he moved out and started the fire.

The sound of Gus' voice startled him. "The Cheyenne were out there most of the night."

"Warn me before you say something, Gus," he pleaded. "What do you think they were doing?"

"I don't know, Tom," he said, "but it was not coming after us or we would be dead now, or the horses would be gone."

"Well, that is comforting to know," Tom said.

With breakfast over it was time to move or hunt. Gus saddled one of the horses and waited for Tom and Hector to do the same.

"We spread out a little and see if we can figure out what the Cheyenne were doing during the night," Gus instructed.

The three men rode forward toward the buffalo carcasses. Gus pulled up and pointed.

"They are butchering our kills," he said.

Several of the carcasses had large pieces of meat removed. Heads were removed from a couple buffalo and several had horns removed.

Gus led them to the rise and sat for several minutes. "How do we tell them it's okay to come and get the meat?" he muttered.

"Follow me, boys," Gus said, spurring his horse ahead. He rode less than a mile in the direction the meat had been taken. They came upon the small herd of buffalo.

Gus swung of the horse and set up to start shooting. Tom followed suit.

"We shoot six buffalo and leave them," he instructed.

Quickly, the animals were put down and the three men rode back to the camp. The wagon was moved three miles west before setting up again to hunt.

The men hunted three more days, managing to harvest 14 hides each day. The next day was Sunday and the Whitestones took the day off.

Tom was restless. When they occasionally sighted the Cheyenne, it felt better than worrying where they were. After the six buffalo were shot for them, the watchers had gone.

He saddled the bay and prepared to do some scouting.

"Stay in sight of the camp, Tom," Gus cautioned.

"I will Gus," he agreed. "I just have to go out there and look around."

The dog followed alongside as Tom rode away from the camp. Tom was glad to have the extra eyes and nose. He rode a mile around the camp while keeping it in sight.

Something caught his eye on a bush beyond the rise. Tom looked at the camp and back at the bush. He would only be a little way out of sight. He looked at the dog and it seemed okay with the direction.

Tom swung off the bay and looked at the bush. What he had seen was a piece of red cloth. He bent down to take a closer look when the dog growled. Tom froze and slowly looked around.

Two braves were standing a short distance away. The Cheyenne stood with spears in hand. Tom's rifle was on the horse and the loop was on his Colt.

"You just don't learn, do you?" he scolded himself. "Now I just might die for it."

The dog was bristling as he stared at the braves. Tom stood, taking his time. He squarely faced the two braves. He was going to draw and throw himself to one side to avoid the spear. With luck, he would get one of the Cheyenne before they got him.

The dog looked back and growled again. There was someone behind him. Tom could feel his skin crawl on his back. He was bracing for the impact of a spear or arrow.

For a moment, Tom wondered if it was okay to cry at time like this. *No*, he decided, *if you have to die, die bravely.*

One of the braves raised a hand, palm out. The dog continued to growl, ready to jump at any time.

"Quiet, dog," Tom said in a stern voice. "You stay!"

The brave removed a claw and tooth necklace with what appeared to be a gold nugget in the middle and held it out to Tom.

"Maybe it isn't your day to die," he whispered.

Using every bit of nerve, he could muster, Tom walked up to the brave and accepted the necklace. Backing away, he put the necklace on and held up his hand palm out.

There was a hint of a smile on the Cheyenne's face. Tom heard a wisp of a sound behind him. The other two braves continued to stand, watching him. The dog was now focused on the two Cheyenne only.

Tom nodded to the men and moved to his horse. Swinging into the saddle, he controlled it with his knees and moved up the rise. At the top, he stopped the horse and looked back. The Cheyenne were gone.

As he turned back to camp, he saw Gus and Hector coming with rifles in hand. Tom raised an arm and waved them back. Trotting the bay, he got back to camp at the same time as the Whitestones.

Gus was angry. "Where the hell did you go?" he demanded.

Tom apologized and then told Gus and Hector about the Cheyenne braves. He showed them the necklace.

Gus sat down, shaking his head. "I don't know if I can take this crap."

A moment later, Gus stood and looked at Tom. "I didn't mean to be so abrupt with you. I guess I was more worried than I wanted to admit. This is good news, Tom. The Cheyenne were thanking us for the buffalo. I don't think we will see this group again."

CHAPTER FIVE

The next week of hunting went well. With the pressure of being watched gone, the men could focus on the work and spend less time looking over their shoulders. Not to say they weren't keeping one eye on the horizon.

The dog was doing a great job of watching. Everyone slept more soundly, knowing that a low growl would warn them of impending danger. And then, as a backup, there was Ralph.

The men continued to move west when hunting. The wagon was almost full. After another week the group would be heading for Fort William. The buffalo, forever on the move, could always be found within a short ride.

The weather was holding nicely. The days were sunny and comfortable, the nights brisk and cold. The men had taken to sleeping with their coats on for warmth. The mature plain grass kept the animals satisfied.

Gus was looking at the distant mountains one Sunday morning. "I have always wanted to see them up close."

Plucking a fat tick off the dog, Tom tossed it into the fire and heard it pop. "We have made good time, Gus," Tom pointed out.

"We could be back in four days," Gus agreed. The decision was made.

Hector was excited about the prospect of getting closer to the mountains. He kept talking about the hunt, the mountains, and wondering what Fort William was like.

Tom watched him pester Gus with questions while the camp was being secured. It reminded him of Isaac. The pain of his brother's loss was still there, but it didn't hurt as much. The dreams of the Vermont farm were fading. Tom did not want to stop dreaming about Isaac and the farm. It was his only chance to be with his brother.

The hunt had brought them to the rolling high plains. Fort William was now to the northeast. The number of buffalo had decreased some, but there were still plenty to finish the load. That would be done as they traveled to the fort.

Preparations for the ride to the mountains were almost done. The hide wagon was hidden near an aspen-covered hillside. They would have to take the horses and mule with them. By switching saddles from one to another, better time could be made. Tom volunteered to ride Ralph.

With enough food for an extra two days, the troop headed west to see the mountains. The rolling hills were covered with goldenrod. The brown grass and other high-country weeds contrasted nicely with the flowers.

There were buttes and foothills to the south, rising from the plain. The mountains loomed purple and majestic to the west. Some of the tops were already covered with snow, giving the promise that winter was not far off.

When Tom saddled the mule, Ralph wanted none of it. He bit and kicked, doing his best to get at Tom. Like the good rider he was, Tom stayed with Ralph and soon had him heading west at a lope.

After the second day of riding, the mountains were still another hard day's ride away. The sun was bright and the air clear. The mountains loomed up in front of them. The men had reached the beginning of the foothills.

The dog had taken after a rabbit around mid-morning. Tom watched the graceful strides as it closed in on the prey. He knew that within a few hours the dog would come back with a bloody muzzle and a satisfied look.

Picking a sun-covered knoll with a good view of the mountains, the trio stopped for a midday meal. Gus sat watching the coffee pot steam over a small fire. "We are close enough. I can now go to my grave saying I have seen the mountains up close."

A hawk rode on the updrafts, searching for unsuspecting prey. They could hear the meadow larks calling to each other. Hector came back from the horses with the coffee.

"How long will it be before the fort?" he asked Gus.

Gus watched Hector measure the coffee in the boiling water. "I figure two weeks, maybe a bit more."

It was late September and the leaves were beginning to show gold. Soon the trees would be bare and the snows would come.

Tom gingerly tasted the hot coffee when they heard a rifle shot. Who was shooting? A Lakota brave rose in the grass not 30 paces away. With a shrill cry, he raised his spear.

Gus shot the Hawken .53 from the hip, hitting the brave squarely in the center of the chest. The Lakota collapsed into a heap. Other braves appeared from the grass ready to charge, giving chilling cries.

The screams of the Lakota ponies caught their attention. Snorting and bucking, the horses were pulling loose from their tethers. Taking a moment to send a few arrows after the fleeing men, the braves turned to catch the horses.

Gus, Hector, and Tom did not wait to see what was happening. Sprinting for their horses, the sound of an arrow clattering harmlessly on some rocks spurred them on.

With extra horses in tow, Gus and Hector headed for some high ground to the south. Tom, astride the bay, missed a grab of the mule's lead rope. Not daring to take a second try, he followed the others at a gallop. Out of range of the arrows, he stopped briefly on a rise to look for the mule. Ralph was hot on his heels, not wanting to be left behind.

Catching the lead rope, Tom cussed the mule. "What the heck were you doing, sleeping? You were supposed to warn us long before they got that close"

He questioned where the dog was. It was probably still chasing the damn rabbit. He wondered who could have shot to warn them. He hoped that whoever it was had got away safely.

Gus pulled up several miles south. The horses needed a breather. A granite wall rose to protect their backs, and some well-placed boulders protected the front.

Hector crouched, wide-eyed, looking at the back trail. Tom knew that Hector expected to see Lakota coming over the plain at any moment.

"We lost the coffee pot and I lost my damn cup," Gus grumbled.

"It was a good shot, Gus," Tom said. "You saved one of us from being run through with the spear."

"Didn't have time to think. Just squeezed off a shot."

Then Tom noticed blood running down Gus' cheek. "Did one of the arrows clip you?"

"Naw," the man replied. "Damn percussion cap flew off the gun and damn near took my eye out."

Feeling safe behind the boulders, Hector said, "Someone has camped here before."

He was pointing at the remains of a small fire to their left. Gus and Tom walked over and looked the area over.

"Well, Tom, tell me what you see," Gus requested.

Slowly, Tom scouted the area. There were a single man's track and a horse. This he told Gus.

Gus nodded. "But look here. The man wears a low-heeled boot. The heel has a circle mark in it. He is not riding, but rather leading the horse. See the placement of the horse's feet? Notice the dragging of the hoofs? It is not a young, but rather an older horse. I would have guessed a tired horse by the tracks, but he was just leaving his camp. It should have been rested, so I figure old."

Tom was impressed. While he read a man and a horse, Gus saw so much more. He knew it was only one man's opinion, yet Tom trusted that it was accurate. He vowed to pay more attention to things around him.

Somewhere in the back of his mind he remembered seeing a boot print with a circle in the heel. Try as he might, he could not think of where. Smiling, he looked up. Gus would have remembered.

Their saddles were switched to the fresher horses and the mule. Riding at a quick trot, the men headed east, taking care not to skyline themselves. The Lakota could very well still be tracking them.

After a sleepless night, the men arrived back at the wagon. Other than a few animal tracks around it, nothing had been touched. Once again Tom had the feeling eyes were on him. With the dog around there would be some warning. But it was gone, left to wander out on the plain, wondering where his people had gone.

The wagon was in a good, defendable location, so the men decided to spend the night and leave for Fort William at first light. With luck, a couple more days of good hunting could be had.

Hector brought out the bean pot to make coffee. The water slowly heated over the small fire. The Dutch oven became their cook pot. They would have to do without biscuits until the fort. Tom was sure that no one would miss them.

"We should have carried an extra coffee pot," Gus lamented. "A man can do without most things, but a good coffee pot he can't."

"Don't you worry, Gus," Hector said cheerfully. "We can afford to get another when we get to the fort."

"Take over a month just to break the damn thing in," Gus replied.

Tom smiled, watching the two brothers interact. He remembered doing the same thing with Isaac.

"We better set up watches tonight," Tom suggested.

"Good idea," Gus agreed. "Not that someone awake will do any good against a determined warrior. At least we will be alerted before we die."

That night, Tom was chased by Lakotas in his dreams. They would rise out of nowhere and come at him. He woke before dawn, covered with a cold sweat. He listened to the morning sounds before he moved. A sound that was missing was the breathing of the dog next to him.

Sitting up, he checked his boots for critters and slipped them on. He put his hat on and checked for his guns. Both were where he'd placed them the night before.

He could see Hector sitting near the wagon wheel. The young man was asleep on watch. For a moment, Tom considered sneaking up and giving him a good scare. The realization that he could get shot doing it made him change his mind. Instead, he coughed a bit as he walked toward Hector.

It was enough. The young man almost jumped out of his skin. "Good morning, Hector."

"Oh, Tom, I think I fell asleep. I sure am sorry. Don't tell Gus," he pleaded.

"He don't have to," Gus snorted. "I have been hearing you snore for the past hour."

After a breakfast of last night's leftover beans and weak coffee, it was time to hitch up and move out. It appeared Hector was having some trouble getting the right amount of grounds into the big bean pot.

At noon, they passed several skinned buffalo carcasses. Tom rode by, looking at the flies and maggots covering the animals. He felt a twinge of regret at the waste he was seeing. He fully understood that when the hunt was over and their wagon moved, someone else would come upon the same scene left by their harvest. He wished that there was a better way.

They woke to large snowflakes the next morning. It was absolutely beautiful to watch. But with the snow came the warning that winter would be here soon.

There was a decent herd of buffalo grazing less than a mile from their camp. Gus sipped his morning coffee.

"It's better this morning, Hector." Looking out at the buffalo, he continued, "We will hunt today and then make a beeline for Fort William. This cold is making my bones ache."

Tom looked at Gus. He estimated that Gus was maybe late thirties or early forties. Hector would be younger than Tom's 24 years. No doubt Gus had lived a hard life. Each morning he would limp around until after morning coffee. Maybe he'd broke too many horses in his younger years, or maybe he'd seen too many fights.

While Tom didn't ask Gus or Hector much about the past, by the same turn he hadn't offered much himself. In the West, Tom had learned, people judged you by what they see in front of them, not what you might have been.

The last hide was folded and tossed into the wagon. The last day's harvest had been 32 buffalo. After a couple days to let them dry, they could finally head for the fort. Tom leaned against the wagon and gratefully accepted the cigar from Gus.

"We've done a heck of a business the past few weeks. Let's have us a good smoke, and then maybe get a couple hours toward Fort Williams before we camp."

Tom took a long puff on the cigar and attempted a ring as he blew out the smoke. His attention was redirected to the barking coming from beyond the wagon. Stepping around, he saw the dog running on three legs, determined to catch up with the men.

Tom squatted to greet the happy mutt. He was given a thorough face licking. Never had Tom seen the dog act like this before. Being lost had changed its behavior.

The front paw had a split pad. The dog had been keeping it clean, but it had made traveling slow. A close inspection revealed some other wounds, mostly healed.

"You had quite a time of it. Looks like you tangled with something pretty mean."

Soon, the dog was resting next to his master, while Tom worked on the cigar. For a moment, all was well with the world.

CHAPTER SIX

Fort William was not really a fort. That is, it was more of a fur trading post with stockade walls. It was located at Laramie's Point on the Platte River. It would eventually be purchased by the U.S. Army and become an important stop on the Oregon Trail as Fort Laramie.

When Gus drove the wagon down, the gate was open, with trappers as well as Indians walking in and out at will. Several structures were built up and down the river. There were a couple clusters of round-topped lodges with black-haired women busy making meals at a central fire.

The leaves had fallen and the maple, birch, and aspen stood with stark, naked limbs. The rich green of the spruce and pine broke the gray-black landscape.

The main store of the trading post was a dim, smoky room. The shelves had most anything a frontiersman could want. One area even had brightly colored beads and trinkets for the ladies. The smell of new leather and rope filled the room.

Tom stopped a moment to look at some steel traps while Gus and Hector walked up to the counter. A grizzled, stocky man was stacking canned goods on a rough plank shelf. He turned to Gus as they walked up.

"The name is Aloysius but I answer to Louie. How can I help you?"

Gus nodded. "This here is my brother Hector and the man looking at the traps is Tom. My name is Gus Whitestone and we have near 300 hides on the wagon outside. They're a mix of young and old. We would like to sell them."

"I certainly can help you with that," Louie smiled. "Let me pour you men a drink before we start business."

Gus and Hector followed Louie across the room to a plank bar. Taking one of the bottles from the back, he poured three brimming shots.

"This here is good rye. I have it brought in from the east." He held one of the drinks out for Tom.

"Just one," Gus warned Louie, "and then we do business."

The count came to 287 hides. Louie offered them $3 each for the smaller hides and $2 for the older large hides. Gus took out the expenses of the venture and the split was $200 per man.

Tom never challenged Gus about expenses. He knew that Gus put up the money and provided for the hunt. Tom didn't even mind if he kept a little extra. Much of his knowledge made the hunts successful.

Louie carefully counted out the money for the hides.

"Keep enough out for a good coffee pot and a couple of extra tin mugs," Gus requested.

The men squinted as they walked into the bright sunshine. The empty wagon stood with the patient team. The sides and floor of the wagon were covered with dried blood and animal fat. The earthy smell of the hides remained in the wagon.

"After we take care of the horses I'll buy us a good supper down at the Buffalo Hide Saloon and Café. Louie is part owner and said it is the best in Fort William," Gus offered.

"As long as it don't smell like this wagon, I'm in," Tom said.

With the horses and mule taken care of in Louie's Livery, it was time to relax. The Buffalo Hide Saloon was located to the west on the river. The sound of ladies' laughter and piano music reached them as the trio navigated their way through the rutted road. The sky was clear and star-studded. The night promised to be a cold one.

Tom was impressed. The Buffalo Hide Saloon had three chandeliers lighting the room. A polished hardwood bar ran along the right wall. Large mirrors were hung on the bar's back wall. The tables sat four to six people and were made by a decent carpenter.

A large-bosomed lady met the men at the door. Her graying-blond hair was piled high on her head. She had a bright red dress and matching ribbons in her hair. One other thing, she smelled good.

"Louie told me you would be coming in. He asked me to buy you men a drink." Turning, she snapped her fingers at the bartender and showed them to a table.

Gus watched her walk away and shook his head. "Either Louie snookered us on the price of the hides, or he is a man that doesn't want to make money."

"I saw some smashed taters in the café when we walked in," Tom said. "I could make a meal out of them alone."

The rye was very good. The woman who greeted them was Lucy. She was Louie's sister. Supper that night was one to remember. Plump, roasted chicken, potatoes, turnips, yams, cornbread, and pumpkin pie for dessert. There was cold milk to drink with the meal, and tea and coffee with the pie.

Lucy made arrangements for the men at a boarding house next door. "No lice, and clean sheets. They will have baths ready for you when you get there."

Gus sat enjoying a glass of brandy. Tom was too full to drink anything at the moment. He just lit up a short, straight cigar called a cheroot. Hector sat staring at the card tables. Many a trapper or hunter had given all his money back at those tables.

"Don't be thinking about sitting at the tables, Hector," Gus warned. "If you feel you got to spend some money, spend it on one of the gals upstairs. At least you will leave with some pleasant memories."

* * *

Tom woke the next morning and the sun was streaming in through the windows. He lay on a feather mattress wearing a new pair of scratchy long johns. The bed sheets were clean and white, and the covers fluffy and warm.

He remembered stumbling into the boarding house late and being directed to a bath. His clothes had disappeared and there were the new long johns and a towel sitting next to the tub of steaming water.

He raised his head to see out the window and the ache began. His head hadn't felt this big since the night he'd met Jinx at the landing on the Ohio River. Tom rolled to the edge of his bed. There were his clothes, washed and folded, sitting on the chair. With a pounding head, he put his clothes on.

The plan had been not to drink, but then he'd tasted the brandy. A check of his money belt revealed that he had spent $17 the night before. It was almost a half month's wages for most folks. Tom realized it could be worse. He could have tried gambling and lost everything.

Pulling on his clothes, he looked out the window and saw the dog lying under some trees in the front of the boarding house. *I best get him something to eat before I leave,* he thought.

Hector and Gus were in the dining room when he came down. Gus was smiling from ear to ear. Hector looked like he might have been hit by the same thing that got Tom.

"Sit down and have some coffee. Breakfast will be right out," Gus boomed.

Tom slumped into a chair and gratefully accepted the coffee.

"You had you a pretty one last night," Gus kidded him.

"Quite frankly, I would prefer if we didn't talk about last night," Tom said.

The coffee was helping to clear his head. Breakfast should have been special. The food looked great, but Tom's stomach wasn't ready to take much on.

"Are you going to winter with us?" Gus asked. "We got a lead on a cabin just downriver. When the thaw comes, we can head out for some prime hides."

"There are some decent hills to the north, and streams that might have some beaver," Tom said. "I figure on buying traps and grub and going after some. Maybe hunt some wolves."

After the men finished, Tom took a couple of thick biscuits and carried them out for the dog. Gus and Hector went to see Louie to let him know they'd take the cabin.

With housing taken care of, the three men stood outside of the trading post with Tom holding the lead rope of the mule. "Are you sure you don't mind selling this long-eared bugger to me?"

"We figure you're going into Cheyenne country and might need more than the dog to warn you," Gus told him.

"Not only that," Hector added. "After a winter with that stubborn cuss, you'll be looking us up to give it back. We'll only take it if you come with it."

Louie heard a chorus of laughter as Tom headed for the stable. He had something he wanted to tell the young man. He might be able to help him with a place to trap this winter.

The trading post owner kept himself busy putting goods away and stirring a pot of soup on his potbelly stove. His sister Lucy liked to bring him something for his midday meal. Louie had also started putting some things together in anticipation of Tom's needs.

The grizzled owner was sitting in the back of the trading post eating off the top of an upturned barrel, a bar rag tucked into his shirt collar, when Tom returned. "Come on back," he called.

"Did you eat anything?" Louie asked as the young man approached.

"The fellow at the livery was eating some bread and cheese," Tom said. "He shared it along with some coffee."

"That's my cousin, Del," Louie said. "Sounds like Lucy has been there also."

Grabbing a three-legged stool, Tom sat across from the owner. "I was hoping you could suggest someplace to trap north of here."

Getting up, Louie went behind the plank bar and returned with two glasses of rye. "I always like a picker up in the afternoon." After setting one in front of Tom, he settled back down. "I got to thinking of old Taggart. He would trap in the winter and fish all summer. The man just didn't like being around folks. Four summers ago, someone found him dead on the side of Clear Creek. He'd been there more than a week and things had started chewing on him."

The stocky owner took a sip of his rye, exhaling in satisfaction. Tom waited and finally asked, "Is that it? Animals chewed on old Taggart?"

"I'm sorry," Louie apologized. "I only allow myself one drink each day and I tend to enjoy the taste as long as possible."

"Anyway," the owner continued. "He had him a fine cabin about five days, maybe a week's ride north of the fort. It's on Beaver Creek. You will cross the Cheyenne River first and then another day or two."

"Does he have relatives around that I can pay to stay there this winter?" Tom asked.

"He left nobody behind," Louie replied. "He was the last of his line. If someone ain't moved in, it will be yours for the taking. I can't see someone wanting to live up that way."

"I need a place to stay with my dog until I leave for trapping," Tom told him.

With Louie's help, Tom moved out of the boarding house and took up temporary residence in a small cabin just north of the fort. It had a small lean-to big enough for the bay and Ralph. The dog took up residence in front of the fire place. His paw had fully healed.

There was much planning to do. Where Tom was heading, there would be no trading post or mercantile. If you forgot to bring an item, you just did without until spring. The young man was pleased when Louie showed him the items he had already pulled together.

Before leaving the fort, Tom rode to Louie's trading post for a last visit to pick up some items he had overlooked. Sitting in front of Louie's was a rundown wagon with the telltale smell of buffalo hides. Sitting on the wagon was a young squaw. Tom only saw her face, which was stunning. The rest of her was covered with a bulky buffalo robe.

Tom nodded at her and rode up to the hitching rail. The morning was brisk, so he hurried into the trading post. He saw a man who must have been the owner of the wagon. The man had sold a few hides and was re-stocking.

"It's a bit cold for your woman out on the wagon," Tom told the man.

The trapper turned to look at Tom. His face was covered with long, dirty, gray whiskers. His stained wool shirt and pants showed the evidence of his livelihood.

"That there ain't my woman. I come by her in a trade. Her pa wanted an old muzzle loader I had. You might call her an investment," he boasted.

"It is still not right leaving her in the cold," Tom replied.

"I tell you what, sonny," the old trapper offered. "I sell her to you and you can make sure she is warm. Hell, it will save me having to feed her this winter. Come spring, I plan to take her to the Green River rendezvous and sell her to one of them mountain men."

Tom did not like the old man, nor the way he talked about the woman. She was a human and he was treating her like cattle. Frustrated, Tom realized that he had butted into something that was none of his business.

"No thank you, I'll pass."

Louie hurried and got the old man's order together and settled up. Hefting his sack of goods onto his shoulders, the old man turned to Tom before leaving. "I will be camped just south on the creek for a couple more days. If you change your mind, let me know. The price will be higher at the rendezvous." Laughing, the old geezer left the trading post.

"It is not right what that geezer is doing, Louie," Tom said.

Louie shrugged his shoulders. "It might not be right, but it is not against the law out here on the plains. In the south, men and women are bought and sold every day."

With the help of the stocky owner, it had taken Tom two weeks to put his packs together. Traps, caps, powder, lead, food, extra blankets and clothes, and a buffalo skin coat. The mule and his bay were in good shape after eating corn and resting.

CHAPTER SEVEN

Gus and Hector came up to see him off. "If you get tired of freezing your butt off, you can always come and spend the winter in our nice warm cabin," Gus chided him.

"Thanks for the offer, Gus," Tom smiled. "Louie told me of a fine cabin about five days ride north along the river. He said there are beaver as big as dogs in the creek."

"Are you going to come back and hunt buffalo with us next spring?" Hector asked.

"I believe my buffalo hunting days are over," Tom said confidently. "After looking at those mountains with you, I have a hunger to go there."

It began to snow big flakes as Tom led Ralph out of the fort and turned north. Gus and Hector followed for a bit, waving and shouting good luck.

The snow didn't slow down. The big, lazy flakes turned to small, hard pellets that stung Tom's face when the wind whipped them around. The dog kept pace with the bay and Ralph. Tom rode until dusk. The snow continued to fall. He was thankful that the wind was light.

Tom huddled near his small fire. The bay and mule were picketed on some sparse grass under the trees. The dog had disappeared to search for food. Tom knew that he would have to try and put together some kind of shelter. The snow had stopped and the open ground was covered with three inches.

He had noticed a large windfall just to the east of his camp. Finishing his supper and leaving the coffee pot on the edge of the coals, Tom went to look it over. The roots had left a large depression in the ground. The upturned root base would protect him from a west wind.

Moving his gear to the windfall, Tom sat in the depression and drank the last of his evening coffee. He smiled as the dog returned. It was carrying a rabbit. Lying next to Tom's feet, it began to eat.

Tom cleared the snow and piled some leaves to spread his bedroll out. With his saddle for a pillow, he was ready for bed. He removed his gun belt and placed it under the saddle. Pulling his boots off and laying the Hawken next to him, he spread his coat over the covers and settled down.

The young maiden's face kept him awake for some time. She'd sat bravely in the wagon, not knowing what her future held in store.

"It just is not right," he muttered.

The weather remained favorable the rest of the ride to the cabin. Tom arrived midday in bright sunshine. A quick appraisal told Tom that Louie may have misspoken about the condition of the cabin.

The door was missing and the center of the roof was severely sagging. Closer inspection revealed that the back wall was pushing out, and the fireplace had crumbled on one side. Tom was pleased to see that the enclosed lean-to was sturdy. It appeared to be later construction.

Tom decided that if the rustic cabin couldn't be fixed he, the dog, horse, and mule would live in the lean-to. The cook fire would be outside. The animals would create adequate warmth in the lean-to.

Winter forage for the animals became the first priority. Tom explored the surrounding area and discovered a meadow with a good stand of brown wild grass. There was little snow on the ground. Tom had brought a long-handled sickle, more commonly known as a scythe. The seasoned grass could be harvested for winter feed.

He also found a valley about a quarter-mile from the cabin. It had only one entrance. The sides could be climbed but were steep. Tom figured that unless the animals were chased, they wouldn't try. The mouth was 200 paces wide. He could put a fence across it to let the horse and mule graze freely.

For two days he worked feverishly using the available aspen trees to build a pole fence across the mouth of the canyon. He also made a crude shelter in the valley for the animals, in case they were caught in a winter storm. Tom's plan was to bring them into the lean-to each night.

The hay that he'd cut in the meadow was stored in the cabin. It would be used in the event of extended foul weather. The animals could be fed in the lean-to.

Tom said his prayers each night, asking for a few more good days to get ready for winter.

Soon, the cabin was half-filled with winter hay. Tom had to stack it around the edges of the room to avoid the gaping hole in the center of the roof.

Quite satisfied with his accomplishments to date, Tom prepared to start setting up a trap line. He had six traps weighing five pound each. The traps had four-foot chains for anchoring. There were three beaver dams Tom had found within two miles of the cabin. Loading traps and stakes onto Ralph, he led the mule toward the first dam. The dog ran with him, ranging out to search for a meal.

Louie had talked about how to place a trap set for the beaver. He had even sold Tom the castor scent to draw the beaver to the trap. The young man wasn't worried. He had trapped in Vermont.

Arriving at the first pond, he saw that it had three beaver lodges and he had heard the splash of a tail as he'd approached. Tom dug into his pack and pulled out a trap. Shaking the chain lose, he knelt on the water's edge with the trap set. He drove a short stake just off the shore to secure the trap. He then pushed it out with a short sapling pole. He reached back to get the container of castor out of his possible bag sitting behind him.

"You are doing it wrong," an unexpected voice said.

Startled, Tom tried to jump up, tripped on the chain and fell headlong into the pond. Spinning around, he surfaced, spitting and coughing water. His soaked revolver would be useless, so he pulled his knife.

Tom sat in two feet of water with his knife in his hand, looking at an old, gray-haired Indian. He tried to get up, but the slope of the pond would not let him. He suddenly felt a sharp pain in his left heel. He thrashed for another minute in the water and finally sat still, looking at the man on the bank.

"I could help you up. But I haven't decided if I am going to kill you or not," the stoic old man said matter-of-factly.

"I think the trap is on my heel," Tom indicated. "I would appreciate you taking it off before I die."

The old, wrinkled face was deep in thought. "It is not a good day to die. I guess I will let you live." The old man reached down to remove the spring trap.

Crawling out of the pond, Tom glared at the mule. "Forget your damn job again."

Water was running off his clothes as Tom got to his feet and stared at the old man. He saw no weapon on the man. He was dressed in leather pants and shirt. His feet were covered with fur-lined boots laced from the sides and ending near the knee. A knee-length deerskin robe covered his shoulders and was tied in the front.

The dripping water began to freeze on Tom's clothing. His heel throbbed from the trap and he was getting chilled. He began to shake.

"Take that mule of yours and follow me. My lodge is very close. It would be a bad thing for you to die of cold and go to the other side knowing so little about trapping."

Tom limped along behind the old man. He heard a growl behind Ralph. The dog had returned from his hunt. *Too late to warn me*, Tom thought.

The lodge was made of buffalo hide stretched over bent poles. There was a hole in the top to allow smoke to escape. It had strange markings on the sides. More hides were placed around the perimeter inside, and a fire smoldered in the center. A blackened and dented pot sat on the edge of the coals with some type of soup.

The morning air was still below freezing. By the time Tom entered the lodge, his clothing had become stiff with ice. He removed his brittle clothes and pulled a buffalo robe lying close by around his shoulders. The old Indian was putting wood onto the fire.

"I am of the Cheyenne people. My Cheyenne name is Néše Méhe. It means Two Buffalo and that is what I go by. Long ago, I scouted for the Army. I learned the language and many of the ways." Two Buffalo rubbed his large nose and continued. "You are in my death lodge. It is my time and I have come here to die as a warrior should."

Still shaking with cold, Tom asked, "Are . . . are you ill?"

"I am old. I eat too much. I will let the young have the food for winter."

Tom looked around the lodge. He could see a bow and some arrows, a knife, and a head dress. Some woven baskets filled with dried berries, corn, and what appeared to be jerked meat, sat near the entrance.

"You had no weapons with you, Two Buffalo," Tom pointed out. "How were you planning on killing me?"

Two Buffalo smiled, his old, weathered face creasing deeply. "I was going to let the cold do that for me."

The Cheyenne dug out two tin bowls and filled them. He handed one to Tom. The mixture of dried fruit and some kind of meat were strange to Tom. The flavor was bland, but it was hot.

The young man's clothing took most of the day to dry, hung on a wooden rack in the lodge. He sat rubbing his ankle and watched the old chief, sitting cross-legged near the fire and mumbling prayers. It was dark by the time Tom was able to dress, his wool trousers just slightly damp.

"It is dark," the Cheyenne suddenly announced, getting up. "You spend the night, and in the morning, I will show you how to set your traps."

Two Buffalo went out to take care of the mule and retrieve Tom's packs. He put the mule into an aspen grove while the dog growled at him, staying a short distance from the lodge.

Two Buffalo returned with the packs. "You have a good dog."

"He does a fine job of keeping an eye out for me when he's not hunting," Tom agreed.

"And he will provide food for a week if necessary," Two Buffalo added.

The young man woke early, only to find the Cheyenne putting wood on the fire. The two of them ate the last of the soup. Two Buffalo handed Tom a pair of moccasins. "Wear these when you go into the water."

First, the old Indian showed Tom places where the beaver left and entered the pond, pointing with a 4-foot walking stick. "Here is where you should set your traps."

To Tom's surprise, Two Buffalo removed his calf-high moccasins and rolled up his britches. His skinny legs and feet were exposed to the cold. Grasping one of the traps, the chief walked into the water and placed the set trap just below the exit the beaver used. He then waded in to the length of the chain and slipped his walking stick through the ring on the end of the chain and drove it part-way into the pond bottom.

Two Buffalo came out of the water to the right of where the trap was set. Rolling down his pantlegs, he pulled on the warm moccasins. Tom then watched him take a stick and push it into the bank above the trap. He then applied some castor to the stick.

Watching the Cheyenne set a proper trap made Tom feel like the pilgrim he was. His first question to Two Buffalo was, "Why not drive the stake near the edge of the pond so you could stay dry?"

Patiently, the chief replied, "Your scent near the trap will keep the beaver away. If you could drive the stake without leaving scent and caught a beaver, it would climb out on the bank to stop from drowning. You would have to fight the angry beaver every time you caught one or if it died, it would be frozen. That is if a wolf or cat didn't find it first."

The explanation was long, but made good sense to Tom. Continuing, Two Buffalo told him,

"Make some poles and find more places to set the rest of the traps. Use the moccasins in the water. I will meet you in the morning and make sure you don't ruin the pelt when you skin it."

By mid-afternoon, two of the ponds had traps set. Tom's feet were numb from entering the water and it felt like he was walking on stumps. He led the mule, heading for the cabin, anxious to check on the bay.

It was dark when Tom got to the cabin. He retrieved the bay from the valley and put it into the lean-to with Ralph. The lonely sounds of wolves and coyotes pierced the night air. There was a chill and the smell of snow.

Tom had rigged up a bunk along the wall. The quarters were tight with the animals, but cozy. The dog came into the lean-to with its head down, growling when he came near. No doubt he could smell Two Buffalo.

A light snow was falling when Tom woke the next morning. Shivering outside the lean-to, he struck the flint to light the fire. Finally, he had the fire going and he placed a pot filled with snow to make coffee. The cabin was located in a stand of aspen. There was plenty of wood, but it burned quickly and would keep Tom busy chopping.

Tom decided to ride the bay to check on the traps. His pulse raced as he discovered that he had caught a beaver in his first trap. Pulling off his boots and socks, he laid them on a burlap bag near the water's edge and put on the stiff moccasins. With his pantlegs rolled up, he waded to the stake that had been pulled over slightly toward the deeper water. Reaching into the water, he grabbed the chain and hauled in his first beaver. He let it lie in the water near the shore as he reset the trap.

Two Buffalo came through the trees carrying a hoop made from saplings. Tom had also made some in anticipation of catches. "I checked earlier and saw that you had caught one," the chief told him. "This area has many beaver. It has been years since the old man trapped here."

Stepping out of the water carrying the 20-pound beaver, Tom stepped on the bag and bent to put it down. "Not in the snow or on ice," Two Buffalo cautioned him. "The fine hair sticks and is pulled off. The fine hair makes the pelt bring in more money."

Tom found a log that had been warmed a bit by the sun and laid the beaver down to start skinning. The chief watch him slit the skin along the belly from nose to tail. Tom worked quickly with his razor-sharp knife and soon had the pelt ready for stretching. Once the pelt was scraped and stretched, Tom stood back.

"It's hard to believe this pelt will sell for almost as much as a buffalo hide," the young man said.

Kneeling next to the discarded carcass, Two Buffalo told him, "I will drain the castor glands in your container." Collecting the castor saved Tom from having to purchase it. Having finished with the glands, Two Buffalo turned to leave. Tom watched as the chief dragged the beaver carcass back to his lodge.

"If I catch more, do you want me to bring them to your lodge?" he called after Two Buffalo.

"You can eat them or use them for bait to catch wolf or coyote."

Tom now had the feeling of success. He was pleased with his first catch. At the second pond he caught two more. Three beavers from the first set left the young man smiling.

He stored the stretched beaver skins in the cabin. The cold temperatures helped in the curing process, preventing decay or loss of hair. It would take about a week on the stretching hoop before the hides would be dry.

The young man cut strips of meat off the carcasses and roasted them for his supper. The beaver meat was a little stronger than Tom was used to, but it would do a good job of supplementing his food.

When Tom set traps for wolf or coyote, he made sure that the dog was in the lean-to. The last thing he wanted was to catch the dog and break its leg in one of the traps.

After a week of trapping and a degree of success, Tom woke to a heavy snow storm. It was impossible to tell the time of day as he went outside, hoping to start a fire. The snow was already six inches deep and if the wind picked up, it would be blinding.

After leading the horses out of the lean-to, he got some hay from inside the cabin and fed them in the shelter of a stand of spruce. He was chilled and wanted something hot to drink. Tom inspected the damaged fireplace. The chimney was clear and it could safely handle a small fire. If the flames were too big and the cabin caught fire, he would lose the catch of beaver as well as his shelter.

Tom also had two wolf skins drying. If the snow slowed a bit, he planned to check the wolf traps and see if he'd caught any more. The young man had found tracks around his cabin and seen wolves slinking through the trees. He kept the Hawken loaded and ready in case a wolf became careless, offering him a shot.

After the sky cleared, Tom donned the buffalo hide coat and led the mule to check the beaver traps. It had been three days since he had been to the ponds. Ice was starting to form due to low temperatures at night. There were several springs or small streams flowing into the pond, leaving plenty of areas open. He found three traps with beaver. Settling on a log, Tom began the job of skinning.

Ralph was restless and snorting. Tom looked around to see if Two Buffalo was near. He was not and the snow-covered hills looked peaceful. It was unlikely that any roving Cheyenne would be out in the snow. Tom turned back to the work at hand.

Protesting loudly, Ralph pulled his lead rope loose and ran past Tom, braying and kicking. Tom jumped up, staring after the mule.

"Get back here, Ralph! You dang fool . . ." His words were cut short by a snarl from behind. Tom turned just in time to glimpse the tawny cougar leap at him. He felt the jaws close on his head as the cat hit him between the shoulder blades. He was knocked forward, twisting as he fell. Tom felt his cap being pulled from his head.

Flat on his back and struggling for breath, he kicked at the cat and slashed with the skinning knife. The Colt revolver was under his coat. Hissing, the cat circled and leaped again. Tom protected his throat with his free arm and drove the knife up at the animal.

Pain shot though his arm as the cat's jaws clamped down like a vice. He stabbed several times at the cat. He could feel the claws tearing at his legs as the cat used its weight to hold him down. Shouting and stabbing at the cougar, he felt his strength leaving him.

Suddenly, the cat snarled and leaped to the side. Tom fumbled for the Colt. It caught on his coat. Jerking it loose, he cocked the gun and brought it to bear on the cougar. It turned, snapping at something on its side.

Tom fired the Colt at the big cat, continuing to squeeze the trigger after it was empty.

"Stop making holes in my hide," Two Buffalo hollered.

Tom looked up at the old Cheyenne standing over him. He held his bow and watched the cat. Tom was shaking from head to foot and everything went black.

He saw the face of the young maiden. She was motioning him to follow. Tom was having trouble focusing on her. He was trying to call to her to wait for him.

Tom woke suddenly to a world filled with pain. His arm and leg throbbed, his back ached, and when he tried to move his head, shooting pains made it impossible to keep his eyes open.

"It was after the beaver," a voice said. "You got in the way."

Slowly opening his eyes, Tom made sure not to move. "What?"

Two Buffalo bent over him, looking into Tom's pain-filled eyes. "The cougar. It wanted the beaver. Good thing I was coming out for meat."

Two Buffalo had taken Tom to his lodge. His wounds were wrapped. Overall, his cuts were not severe. The buffalo coat had done a good job of protecting him from the teeth and claws. The blow when the cat had hit Tom, and the powerful bites, had caused a lot of bruising.

"I can imagine the cat's surprise when he grabbed for your head and came away with a mouth full of cap," Two Buffalo chuckled.

"How long have I been here?" Tom asked.

"Two days only. I found the mule at your cabin and put it in the lean-to with the horse. Your dog has been snapping at me every time I went to water and feed the animals."

Tom carefully raised himself to his elbow. Next to him, he could see the beaver pelts scraped and stretched on hoops. Beyond the firelight was a large, tawny hide drying on a frame. Two Buffalo had removed the claws and was making a necklace. He filled a bowl with meat and broth for Tom.

The broth was hot and good, and the meat tender. "You do a good job with beaver."

"Beaver, bah! You are eating cougar. Some of the best meat you can find," Two Buffalo informed him.

It turned out that his knife had done little damage to the cat and he had only hit it twice with the Colt, neither one being kill shots. Two Buffalo's well-placed arrow had been the end of the cougar.

Tom had a gash on his scalp, claw marks on his legs, and puncture wounds on his arm. The wounds healed well with Two Buffalo's remedies. It would take stretching and time to loosen the bruised muscles.

Within a few days, Tom was up and around. While Two Buffalo's lodge was cleaner and smelled better than the lean-to, he was happy to be back in his own bed.

Soon, the ponds were frozen over and the beavers were feeding in their lodges. Tom kept a few traps in the swifter moving water to catch the wandering animal looking for tender branches. He would catch an occasional beaver.

January brought two blizzards that kept Tom indoors for several days at a time. The howling wind forced snow into every crack of the lean-to. The breath of the mule and horse hung thick on the cold air. Tom spent the days curled up in his bunk with his blanket, the buffalo coat, plus the bay's horse blanket covering him. The dog curled up near the bay, sharing the body heat.

With the ponds frozen over, Tom focused on his trap line. By the end of February, he had managed to catch six wolves, a fox, and four coyotes. He had a total of 27 beaver pelts. Two Buffalo kept the cougar hide. It would be his death robe.

Often Tom would spend the day in Two Buffalo's lodge and listen as the chief told him stories of hunts and battles. While regaling him with the stories, he also showed him how to make snow shoes. Using aspen poles, they also made snow snakes to slide along the crusted snow in completions.

The snow in the woods was over two-feet deep. Tom was using the snow shoes he'd made with the chief. While following his trap line for wolves, he stopped suddenly.

The ground around his trap was trampled and splattered with blood. Cautiously, he approached the trap. His bait was gone as well as his prey. All that was left in the trap was a wolf foot left behind by the rest of the pack.

Looking up, Tom caught sight of something moving through the trees. He wasn't sure if it was his imagination or a wolf. He turned back toward the cabin. Soon he noticed that something had used his snowshoe packed trail. Closer inspection confirmed that it was wolf tracks!

Tom moved his Colt from the holster to his buffalo coat pocket. Vivid memories of being attacked by the cougar returned.

"If a wolf jumps me, I will have the Colt ready," Tom vowed.

Two Buffalo and Tom also spent many hours together snow shoeing in the hills or on the plain. Tom learned much about the various tracks and sign from Two Buffalo. Time was spent talking about ways to determine direction on cloudy or snowy days. At night, Two Buffalo pointed out stars that could be used as a guide.

Winter survival was a constant topic. Tom learned to make a shelter by pulling dense brush or evergreens together and then weaving branches in the sides. If caught in the open, he could cut and stack blocks of snow for a wind break. While Tom was aware that it could be fatal to allow sweating in frigid weather, Two Buffalo still spent time warning him about it.

Edible roots and tubers were dug from the frozen ground or icy bottoms of ponds. Two Buffalo demonstrated making fish traps and weapons out of available plants and trees.

A mid-March storm caught the two men near the cabin. Tom was able to convince Two Buffalo to spend the night. Tom moved his packs around to make more room for sleeping.

"The smell of your animals is strong in your lodge," Two Buffalo complained.

"The warmth they provide makes up for the smell," Tom pointed out.

While placing one of the packs, it fell over, spilling some of its items. The necklace Tom had received out on the plains fell out.

Picking it up, Tom showed it to Two Buffalo. He saw Two Buffalo's eyes go wide.

"Where did you get that?" Two Buffalo demanded.

"It was given to me by some Cheyenne out on the plains," Tom answered, confused.

"You have a powerful medicine necklace. It would only be passed due to the death of its owner or by rewarding an extraordinary deed."

Tom told Two Buffalo about the events that led to being given the necklace. Two Buffalo nodded and grunted while Tom talked.

"Some of the tribes in the south have had many of their warriors and hunters killed by the white soldiers. They have also been attacked by other tribes looking for horses or scalps," Two Buffalo said. "This group was probably facing starvation and maybe freezing this winter. The buffalo you shot must have saved them. This act of kindness no doubt moved them greatly."

"I hadn't thought," Tom said, looking at the ornate necklace.

"Wear it and let others see it. The necklace will protect you," Two Buffalo advised. "But be warned, others will fight you to possess it."

Tom carefully put it back into the pack. He questioned whether he was truly worthy of being given the necklace.

One clear and cold March day, Tom put the bay and mule into the pasture. He went back to the lean-to clean out the stall. He had quite a pile of manure behind the building from the animals. Once finished, Tom put a new edge on his axe. Soon, he was chopping wood in his shirt sleeves, steam rising from his back. Being close to his shelter, Tom didn't worry about perspiring and just enjoyed the strenuous workout.

The dog stood suddenly, looking toward the pasture and barking. At almost the same moment he heard the braying of the mule and the bay's shrill scream.

Dropping the axe, Tom scooped up his holster and Colt lying on the woodpile. The braying and screams of the animals became continuous. The dog disappeared in front of Tom, heading toward the commotion.

Tom could see the animals surrounded by wolves, fighting for their lives. Both were doing their best kicking and biting at the gray killers. The dog got to the animals first, and in a fluid movement launched into the side of one of the wolves.

Tom could see two wolves had the hind quarters of the bay hamstrung, attempting to bring it down. In desperation, Tom brought the Colt up and shot at one of the wolves hanging on to the bay.

Quickly, he emptied the Colt on the attacking wolves and then realized he was now without a weapon. It had been enough. The wolves ran for the hills with the dog on their heels. The mule looked after the departing wolves, still braying loudly. The bay stood shaking, with blood dripping from its flanks, spattering bright red onto the winter snow.

Three wolves lay dead, one from the accurate feet of the mule and two from Tom's now empty Colt. He shouted for the dog to come back. Tom slung the holster over his shoulder and took the two animals by the halter and headed for the lean-to.

Tying Ralph next to the lean-to, Tom turned his attention to the bay. Its flanks had deep grooves where the eye teeth of the wolves had raked it. A quick inspection told Tom that the damage was not severe. He wiped the cuts and applied some grease to keep them moist.

Behind him, he heard the heavy panting of the dog returning. A quick look told him that the dog had gotten the best of the wolves without serious damage.

Tom reloaded the Colt and Hawken rifle. Suddenly feeling chilled, he put on his buckskin coat. Walking back to the pasture, he was hoping to get another shot at the wolves. The Hawken .50 caliber would do a fine job on them.

He entered the area and the wolves were back, tearing at one of the carcasses. Tom brought the Hawken up, but before he could line up on one, the wolves disappeared into the trees. The dog charged, growling, but stopped just short of the trees. Tom brought a piece of rope to drag the dead wolves back for skinning.

The warm breeze of spring began to blow in April. During the winter outings with Two Buffalo, Tom had found two more ponds on some of the smaller streams and he had set traps in them. The beaver he'd caught still had thick, prime coats.

The fear of hungry wolves had limited the amount of time Tom put the animals into the pasture. He was enjoying watching the horse and Ralph run around the valley pasture with their tails flying. The dog found a sunny bank to sleep on. He would open an eye and watch Tom or Two Buffalo walk by, unmoving in any other way.

"Your dog no longer snaps at me," the chief said, smiling. "He knows winter is over and he is safe from the cook pot."

Laughing, Tom agreed. Secretly, he hoped that the dog hadn't decided to accept Indians as friends. He still needed him to be a watch dog.

"I will be leaving soon for the June rendezvous. There I will sell my furs and resupply before going into the mountains."

Tom saw a flash of sadness cross Two Buffalo's face.

"I am glad I decided not to kill you. It made me feel useful teaching you things and in turn you fed me well. I will miss seeing you each day."

Tom smiled at his winter friend. He had learned much from Two Buffalo. They were important things for surviving as a mountain man.

Twice his life had been saved by Two Buffalo, if he counted the time the chief decided not to kill him.

The time to leave was getting close. Tom had pulled his traps for the season and had a young beaver hanging from the mule's saddle horn. He would be going to the rendezvous with 32 beaver pelts, plus the other skins. He had nothing to gauge his catch with, but Tom felt that it had been a good winter.

He approached the lodge from the back and came around the side and froze. He came face to face with four Cheyenne. One of the braves glared at him and shook a lance adorned with feathers and beads. Tom's Colt was in its holster, hanging on the saddle horn with the beaver. He had nothing but his knife to defend himself with.

Before he had a chance to pull the knife, Two Buffalo emerged from the lodge. The chief and the angry Cheyenne had tense words and the brave kept pointing the end of the lance at Tom. Trusting his friend, the young man kept his hand away from his knife, not wanting to provoke the angry brave further.

The four Cheyenne had their horses tied just beyond the lodge. Suddenly, the angry brave turned and was followed by the other three. Leaping on their horses, they galloped away, the angry brave coming close to Tom and tapping him with the end of his lance.

Tom stood confused by the confrontation. He was thankful that the brave had only tapped him with the feathered end and not run him through with the lance. Two Buffalo walked up to his friend. "They came to my lodge to bury me. They expected to find me dead after the cold winter."

"Why were they angry?" Tom asked. "The braves should have been happy to find you alive and well."

"The angry brave wanted to find me dead. It would open a seat on the council for him and he would then be a chief," Two Buffalo said. "You saw his disappointment."

The day was warm and large patches of snow had melted. Tom invited the chief to join him at his cabin for a meal of beaver meat. Neither spoke of the young man's leaving. Tomorrow, Tom would start packing the pelts and skins for traveling. He was going to head straight to the rendezvous without stopping at the fort.

After two days the packing was finished. Tom and Two Buffalo sat in the death lodge and shared a last meal of soup made with cattail roots, some early greens, and the meat from a rabbit that the chief had shot. The next day Tom would be leaving.

"You spoke to a woman after being attacked by the cougar. You had not yet come back to our world."

Tom nodded. "I saw the face of a young Indian girl in my dream. She wanted me to come with her."

"You will meet her again and she will be yours," Two Buffalo shared with Tom. "It came to me in a vision. It will be so."

"I would like that, Two Buffalo."

Tom picked up a small pack he had brought to the meal. He removed the necklace that had been given to him.

"You said this necklace would only be given upon death or after receiving great kindness," Tom said, handing the necklace to Two Buffalo. "You have been a true friend and teacher this past winter. You also saved my life. I would be honored if you would be accepted this necklace."

With shaking hands, Two Buffalo took the necklace and placed it around his neck. "I will wear this for you. I will ask the great spirit to protect you in your travels."

Tom looked at his friend with admiration. During the first meeting, he had seen an old man waiting to die. He now saw the spark of life in Two Buffalo's eyes and truly the will to live.

The next morning, with the furs and his gear packed on Ralph, Tom rode the bay southwest toward the Green River. He looked back and waved at Two Buffalo, who was standing and watching him ride away.

For the second time in his life, Tom felt the pain of loss. The first time was when he'd left the cove that Isaac was buried in, and now leaving a true friend, never to see him again.

Tom would not be returning to this part of Wyoming. He had dreams of higher mountains and new, exciting places to see. Hunting buffalo offered a way to earn money. Seeing the wasted carcasses on the plains bothered Tom. What he did with his life had to be more than just money. It had to include seeing new vistas.

The plain was covered with spring flowers. The seemingly endless expanse of green grass with patches of dark sagebrush and dotted with blue, purple and yellow flowers fulfilled some of the yearning in Tom. It drew him forward, filled with excitement to see over the next rise or around the next bend.

Tom spent the first night next to a small stream. The bay and Ralph grazed hungrily on the tender grass. The dog lay watching him set up camp. After building a small fire, Tom filled the coffee and soup pots from the stream.

He set them to heat next to the fire. Walking along the stream, Tom found wild onions and tender ferns. At home they had called them fiddle heads. Returning to the fire, he added some beans, the last of his side meat, and the wild onions to the steaming pot of water. He measured grounds into the boiling coffee pot.

Watching the new grass wave in the wind, and seeing the white clouds against the blue sky, gave Tom a true feeling of peace. The smell of his coffee drew Tom's attention and he poured a cup to enjoy while he waited for the soup.

He added the fiddle heads to the pot and a bit more salt just before getting ready to eat it. The beans had thickened the broth enough to make it very hardy. The tender fiddle heads made it special.

"Hello, the fire!" a fellow traveler called.

Tom stood and loosened the Colt in his holster. Dusk was setting in, and he couldn't clearly see the rider.

The man was riding a buckskin and leading a brown packhorse. He appeared to be of medium height and was dressed in dark wool pants and a plaid wool shirt. He had a short beard and a sagging, round-topped hat. He carried a Hawken rifle in the scabbard on his horse and a large knife on his hip.

"Climb down and have a seat," Tom called back. "I just finished making supper. You're welcome to join me."

"Don't mind if I do," the man thanked Tom. "I could smell your coffee for the last half-mile."

The man reached his hand out. "They call me Chess Handlin."

Tom introduced himself and accepted the bowl Chess had brought with him. He filled it with the hot bean soup. Tom then filled the man's cup with coffee.

"Are you heading for the rendezvous?" Chess asked.

"Yes, I am," Tom answered.

Chess got up and headed for his horse. Tom moved his hand to his Colt. Digging in his pack for a moment, the man returned with a bundle wrapped in a cloth.

"I got some biscuits here. They're a couple days old, but should soak up well in the soup," Chess said, offering Tom some.

Chess had noticed Tom's hand had been resting on the Colt. Taking a couple of biscuits, Tom sat back to enjoy the meal.

It was full dark when supper was done. The biscuits may have been two days-old, but they tasted every bit as good as Hector's fresh ones.

Chess wiped his mouth with the back of his hand. "I am going to put my horses up. We rode far today and they need a rubdown."

Tom noticed that he was being a little more direct in his moves. It was probably because Tom had been jumpy earlier. The young man knew it paid to be watchful with strangers.

"Let me help you," Tom offered.

CHAPTER EIGHT

Two days out of Green River, Tom and Chess came across a single set of wagon tracks. It had been coming from the north before turning west to the rendezvous.

Tom swung down and took a closer look at the tracks. "I wouldn't be surprised if these were made from a rundown hide wagon I saw last fall in Fort William. I noticed a loose rivet on a back wheel. This one leaves such a mark in the track."

"If these were their tracks, they're about two days-old," Chess estimated.

"I agree," Tom nodded. "That would put them at the rendezvous about now."

Tom continued to watch the wagon trail to determine if it was the old geezer and if he still had his passenger. When they came to the wagon's night camp, Tom motioned Chess to stay back for a minute. Carefully, he read the sign.

He found small, bare footprints that could have been the young maiden. It appeared that she might be tied up part of the time. Another set if tracks were never far from her. Now he knew it was the old geezer.

Chess came up and looked the camp over. "Don't look like he trusts her much."

"I read it the same. I found some pigging strings that had been cut off her wrists. Probably ties her up when he sleeps."

"Did you see this?" Chess asked, pointing to the ground.

"I did," Tom said, his jaw firm. "It looks like she is dragging some kind of chain on one ankle."

It was too early to make camp. Tom was glad to move on. The girl was being treated like an animal, or a criminal. He could read her discomfort everywhere around the camp.

Chess pointed out a clump of willows an hour before sunset and turned his horse toward it. "It's got water and grass. Another day's ride and we should be at the Green River."

Tom pulled the gear off his horse and mule. He could see the dog taking a long drink at the stream. Tomorrow, he would find out if the old geezer still had the girl or if he'd sold her the first couple of days. Tom shook his head. He didn't want to think that.

"Mind if I make supper tonight?" Chess asked, holding up the two prairie chickens he had shot.

"It would be a pleasure eating cooking other than my own." Tom began to put a fire together from the ample branches under the willows.

Chess pulled out his Dutch oven and made up sourdough biscuits. He had some honey to pour on the hot biscuits. The prairie chickens were tender and juicy, and the coffee was hot and strong.

Sitting alone near the fire, Tom checked the amount in his money belt. He still had $210. He quickly put it away when he heard Chess come back from relieving himself. Tom wondered if that would be enough money to make a deal with the old geezer.

Tom had decided he would purchase the young Indian girl and then bring her back to her people and give her freedom. The only problem, he realized, was that her father had traded her away once and might do so again.

Tom fell asleep and dreamt about the young maiden. He woke at first light. The night sky had been clear and there was frost on the ground. A thought had come to mind during the half-sleep just before he woke up. Was his quest for the young girl because of the loss of his brother? He did not fully understand why it felt so important to find her.

Tom got up and added some wood to the hot ashes. He then hurried to the stream to fill a pot of water. The wood was smoldering as he carried the pot of water back. He splashed some on his pant leg and swore softly.

He was blowing on the coals to help the wood catch fire when Chess rose up on one elbow. "You sure are in a hurry this morning," he chided Tom.

"I am heating some water to wash up and shave," Tom said, as he sat back with satisfaction as the flames licked at the wood.

"I expected you would take a bath all over in that there stream, knowing you expected to meet someone special at the rendezvous," Chess kidded.

"Thought about it," Tom stated, "but it is just too damn cold."

It was an hour after sunup and the two men rode out from the willows. Tom's cheeks were stinging from the shave he had given himself.

"You sure do clean up good," Chess laughed.

Tom was happy Chess had caught up with him. Riding alone was a lonesome way to travel. He could talk to his horse or Ralph. He could even talk to the dog, but none of them answered back.

Chess had been to a rendezvous before and he painted a pretty exciting picture of what Tom could expect. Other than the drinking and gambling, there would be wrestling, shooting, and knife throwing contests.

There would be displays of all the latest hunting and trapping gear. Also available were blankets, clothes, footwear, cooking pots, saddles, saddlebags, tobacco, and other types of personal items.

The rendezvous had been started by General Ashley in 1825. It was known as the Rocky Mountain Rendezvous. It had been held at Green River, near Horse Creek, Wyoming, since 1835 with one exception. In 1838, it had been held at the Popo Agie in Wyoming.

What Tom and Chess did not know was that this was to be the last Rocky Mountain Rendezvous. The demand for beaver pelts had dropped, replaced by silk for hats, and the number of mountain men had decreased. The Hudson Bay Company was undercutting the prices of supplies to draw the mountain men away from the American Rendezvous system.

The men stopped on the rise overlooking the winding Green River. It was the end of June. Smoke from many fires rose in the afternoon sky. The mountains rose magnificently in the west. Below them was the rendezvous. There were groups of Crow, Shoshone and other tribes, with their lodges scattered across the valley, far outnumbering the trappers.

The mountain men set up lean-tos, purchased teepees, or rigged other temporary quarters. Some just used a buffalo skin over their wool blankets. Two large, colorful tents were in the middle, which housed the American Fur Trading company. Other suppliers of goods were scattered along the river. The rendezvous spread a couple of miles in each direction.

Tom wondered if he would see Jim Bridger, Joe Walker, or even Kit Carson. Chess believed that Joe Meek would be there.

Tom was overwhelmed looking at all the camps where trappers and Indians were spread across the valley. The only women came with the Indians, other than a few traveling with the missionaries. He worried if he would find the old geezer or the young maiden he had dreamt so much about.

Chess recommended a campsite upstream from the main festivities. "Better water there."

A Shoshone gave them the chance to purchase a sagging teepee located near a large oak. It was better than sleeping under the stars. The location had plenty of grass for the stock.

Once they had the horses taken care of and their gear stored in the teepee, the two men walked toward the large trading tents. There were discussions about the low price of beaver pelts. Some years back the men would get $5 a beaver and now it was down to $2 for prime pelts.

Tom did not care about the prices. He was here for the experience of being among so many other mountain men. The trading tent exceeded his expectations. How all this stuff was brought overland from Westport, Missouri for the rendezvous was beyond his comprehension.

A bar was set up in one tent. It consisted of wooden planks on some empty crates. There was lots of rye, and even some champagne for those who wanted the best.

Tom bought some cigars and headed for the bar to join Chess. The rye burnt nicely down his throat. It had been a long, dry winter. Offering a cigar to Chess, the two leaned back against the bar and watched the activity.

He had visited a fair back in Vermont when he was 12. Tom remembered seeing people everywhere buying, selling, and mostly eating. He had thought that it was the most exciting thing he would live to see.

The rendezvous had the fair beat by far. There was something untamed at this gathering. It had earthy, unclean exhilaration, the feeling that anything could happen or be had, and probably would. Nothing was off limits.

He arrived back at the camp well after dark. Tom's head was spinning from both the rye and everything he'd seen going on. Chess had met some old friends who were going after some wild nightlife and had asked Tom to join. Using his better judgment, Tom had declined.

Tom sat near the fire drinking some hours-old coffee. He leaned against an oak tree and watched the glowing end of his cigar. In the distance, he could hear the shouts and laughter of men. There was an occasional report of gunfire. The dog, uncomfortable with all the celebrating, lay close to his master.

The sun found Tom lying on his side next to the spreading oak. His mouth was dry and his head throbbed to the rhythm of his heart. He tried to move and heard the growl from the startled dog lying close to him.

Sitting up, he looked around the camp. Chess had not made it back. The horses were standing at their picket ropes, waiting to be watered and moved. The fire he had started last night was now cold.

"First things first," Tom muttered. Slowly, he got up and went to tend to the horses.

He was finishing his coffee when Chess returned to the camp, his clothing soiled and sporting a nice black eye. Tom noticed he was smiling from ear to ear.

"You had a good night, Chess," Tom said.

"It was a night to remember, Tom," he replied. "I got to sleep for a couple hours. When I get up, ask me about the old geezer."

Chess ducked into the teepee and stumbled to his blankets. He was soon snoring.

Tom wandered around the gathering. In the morning light, things were a bit different. The grass was trampled to dust, or mud if near the river. Camps with personal gear were spread everywhere. Latrines had been dug, but many a drunken trapper didn't make it there, so you had to watch where you stepped. All in all, Tom still found it exciting.

The smell of roasting buffalo drew Tom to a tattered tent. A heavy-set man with bulging jowls was uncovering a pile of juicy meat that had been buried over coals the night before.

The man looked up at Tom, exposing an impressive goiter. "I got some mighty fine buffalo here," the man boasted. "You could be the first customer."

Tom's queasy stomach from the night before had settled with his morning coffee. "I believe I will."

The juicy meat was put into a birch bark container that the big man had contracted some Flathead women to make. Tom paid for the meat and walked back to a place where he had noticed a man making bread in a stone and clay hearth.

Tom returned to the camp with the juicy roasted buffalo and a couple of loaves of warm, baked bread. Chess was sitting in front of the teepee, rubbing his head.

"I got us some food fit for royalty here," Tom bragged.

Chess groaned and tilted his head back, his eyes still closed. "Coffee first, please."

Tom stoked up the fire and put coffee water on. He then slit one of the loaves of bread and filled it with the tender buffalo meat.

Chess watched through his good eye as Tom made short work of the meal.

The dog sat watching the other container intently. "You stay out of that meat," Tom warned the animal.

Adding some coffee grounds to the boiling water, Tom sat back and reminded Chess, "You told me to ask you about the old geezer."

Nodding, the man poured himself a cup of coffee. "Yes, I did find out a thing or two."

Sitting back with a grunt against the oak tree, Chess sipped the scalding coffee.

"What I learned earned me this black eye." He started touching the eye gently. "I was coming back from having some fun with the friends I ran into. We had enjoyed some rye and women folk down by the river."

"I heard some fiddle music coming from south of the big tent. Figuring one more drink couldn't hurt, I was drawn to it. There, on the edge of the crowd, was this feisty old man. He had this young Arapahoe gal with him and was dickering with two men.

"Having all the courage of the rye I had been drinking, I walked up and told him he couldn't sell her because she was spoken for. You would have thought I had broken wind at a church social. The two men and the old geezer were all over me. By the time I had my wits about me and got up from the ground, they had disappeared."

Tom poured himself coffee and absorbed what Chess had said. "How long before you got back here?"

"Well, it was just about light when I came across them. I stopped and had another rye or two on the way back for the pain."

"When your stomach lets you, have some of the meat and bread. It is good eating."

Warning the dog away from the meat again, Tom checked his Colt and headed for the area Chess had described.

Tom recognized the rundown hide wagon first. The old geezer had made camp south of the trading tents, under a grove of cottonwood.

The first thing he saw was the young Arapahoe girl, or more correctly, the young woman. She sat on a log near the fire, staring straight ahead. Tom was struck by how proud she held herself. Her black hair was put up into two braids. She squinted a bit with her brown eyes, looking into the distance. Her full lips were parted just a bit.

She was wearing a new gingham dress that was probably purchased at the trading tent. Her figure was well-defined by the way the dress followed her curves. Her feet were still without shoes or moccasins.

Tom had noticed some chafing on one ankle just below the hemline of the dress, which was no doubt from the shackle and chain she had worn.

Just beyond the fire, the old geezer was stowing some things in his pack. As Tom passed the woman to talk to the old geezer, she glanced at him. He saw something in her eyes. He wondered if it might have been recognition from seeing him before.

The old geezer noticed him walking up. "Something I can help you with?" he asked.

"Yes, there is," Tom answered. "I have come to talk to you about the Arapahoe woman."

Shrugging his shoulders, the old geezer turned back to his packs. "Talk all you want. She don't belong to me no more. Two Mexican fellows made a deal with me this morning. They're trading their furs right now and will be bringing me back the money."

Tom felt like he had been kicked in the stomach. He was too late. In desperation, he asked the old geezer, "How much did they offer you?"

"I'll be getting $500 for my investment. Eva here was a lot of trouble to get this far, but it is going to pay off now."

That was it, Tom knew. He would have barely over that when his furs were sold and still needed to purchase supplies for the coming fall and winter.

Tom mumbled thanks to the old geezer and headed back for his camp. He walked behind the young woman, not wanting to look into her eyes again. He now had a name with the face, for all the good it would do.

Chess tried his best to cheer Tom up. There was a rifle shoot coming up that afternoon and it took some encouragement to get Tom to it.

Clay mugs were set up on a log 10 paces down range. Twenty-seven men showed up for the shoot. The winner would get two bottles of rye.

"See, what I told you, Tom." Chess said, beaming. "You win this and that should be enough liquor to make you forget about your troubles."

Tom smiled at Chess and truly appreciated his attempts to change his mood. Although it had only been a couple of hours since Tom had found that Eva was out of his grasp, already the merriment of the rendezvous was lifting his spirits.

Tom was the 18th man to shoot. He loaded the Hawken. Sighting on the clay mug, he squeezed off a shot. The rifle recoiled in his hands and the mug shattered into pieces. There were 12 men left after the first round.

The next mugs were set up at 25 paces. Tom shot second. A breeze had picked up from right to left. The first shooter had missed the mug to the left. Tom adjusted slightly for the wind and squeezed off his second shot. Again, the mug shattered.

Chess had survived the first round but missed his second shot. He slapped Tom on the back. "It's up to you, partner. Go get us that rye."

The words struck Tom. Chess had called him his partner. How many others had he partnered up with since leaving Vermont? Acquaintances could come and go quickly on the frontier. Partnering up was more often for convenience and safety during travel rather than sticking with a friend.

"Your turn again, Tom," Chess told him.

His attention back on the contest, Tom saw that the mugs were now 100 paces downrange. Hitting a four-inch wide target without a fixed rest at that distance would be as much luck as skill.

There were five men left shooting. The first two men missed. One shot short and the other's shot echoed into the hills, ricocheting off a boulder well behind the target. Tom stepped up to the line.

His Hawken rifle had rifling. It would spin the ball, making the flight truer. He kneeled, looking downrange at the mug. Resting his elbow on his knee, he did his best to adjust for the drop and wind. The Hawken had two triggers. The back one set the hammer on the front trigger. The front had a hair trigger action.

Tom set the action with the rear trigger. Letting the tension go from his shoulders, he lined up on his target and touched off the forward trigger. The rifle recoiled and for a split-second the mug stood still, and then exploded into fragments.

A cheer went up from the crowd as Tom stood up and walked back to Chess with a grin that almost hurt, it was so wide.

The last two men missed in turn and Tom was declared the winner of the two bottles of rye. Picking up his prize, Tom and Chess walked toward the camp. Chess was inspecting one of the bottles.

"Hot damn, Tom," he exclaimed. "This isn't rye, this here is fine brandy."

Tom laughed, "Well, Chess, I recommend you and I each pack one of these away for cold nights in the mountains."

Tom saw the old geezer while trading his pelts and skins next day. The man was pretty well liquored up and enjoying his gains on his investment.

The beaver brought the expected $2 per pelt. He got $30 for the other skins. He saw a trapper get $80 for a cougar skin that was smaller than the one that attacked him. He smiled and thought of Two Buffalo.

He decided to put off the purchase of supplies for a couple of days. Tom liked the feel of a full money belt. He saw a group of men shooting handguns. They had a group of targets set up at 10 paces and were betting on hitting what they shot at.

Tom joined in. The going bet was $1 per shot. The shooter had to cover the other bets. Tom had done a fair amount of shooting with the Colt and generally hit what he aimed at.

A few of the men liked to see how fast they could pull their gun and shoot. Tom, like most, wore his Colt high on his hip and it wasn't set up for speed. Rather than aiming the Colt at a target, Tom found that when he pointed it like a finger at a target, he had the most success.

Tom bet against the shooter the first two times, lost one and won one. He was content to be even. He volunteered to shoot. A few men who saw him shoot the Hawken didn't put up any money. Tom ended up having to cover eight bets.

Tom pulled the Colt and held the gun with the barrel toward the sky. He chose a beaver skull stuck on a stick. Shaking his shoulders, he stood facing the target. Dropping the Colt level, he squeezed the trigger. The gun bucked in his hand and the beaver skull skipped off the top of the stick.

For the next hour Tom enjoyed the friendly betting. He was a few dollars ahead. One disgruntled loser pushed his way to the shooting line when Tom was taking bets.

"You think you're a hotshot, don't you? Let's see how you do shooting against another man."

For a moment, Tom thought the man wanted to brace him and shoot it out, duel style. He was relieved when the man pointed at two low bushes just over 25 paces away.

"The first one that shoots three branches off his bush wins," the man challenged.

Tom had seen the man around. His name was Calvin Ward, and he tended to be a disagreeable cuss. Tom had witnessed him beating up more than one lesser opponent.

"Calvin, I will take your challenge. The only thing is we load six shots in our weapons and, at the end of six shots, the one that has knocked the most branches off wins."

Calvin was a stocky and smelly trapper dressed in dirty buckskins. One could say he had a beard, but it was obvious he just didn't bother shaving.

"We shoot for $20 for the most branches. These galoots behind us can make side bets," Calvin stipulated. It was obvious that he wanted final say on the rules.

Stepping up to the line, Calvin spit a stream of tobacco juice, coming pretty damn close to Tom's boots. Tom finished loading all the chambers in his Colt and joined Calvin.

Calvin snapped at a man standing to the side, "You there, say when to start."

Both men stood with their holstered guns, waiting for the signal.

"Now!"

Calvin grabbed for his gun, his first shot hitting the dirt halfway to the target as he drew. Tom pulled his Colt nearly as fast, hesitating for a split-second to line up on his bush.

With his Colt at waist level, Tom fired rapidly at the bush, clipping five branches off. Calvin had finished shooting before Tom had fired the fifth time. He had hit only three branches.

"You changed the damn rules in your favor," Calvin scowled, as he threw two $10 gold pieces onto the ground in front of Tom.

Tom felt his muscles tense. The man had now pushed him twice, once spitting and now making him pick the money off the ground while insinuating he didn't play fair.

The two men stood staring at each other with empty guns. "If you think different rules would favor your shooting, call them now and we'll go for double or nothing," Tom said coldly.

Tom's fist was clenched, and suddenly he wanted the son-of-a-lowlife to make a move. Their eyes locked for a moment and then Calvin grunted and walked away.

Tom knew that this wouldn't be the end of Calvin Ward. The challenge Tom had given was too even and Calvin liked an advantage. The foul man had originally thought rapid shooting would favor him.

The rest of the men cheered Tom's winning and a short, stoop-shouldered man bent down and picked up the gold pieces for Tom.

"Watch that Calvin Ward," he warned Tom. "He is a back stabber if I ever saw one."

The men continued shooting and betting for most of another hour before the competition broke up. Tom was still ahead a few dollars, plus the gold pieces.

Chess was working on supper when Tom got back. "I heard about you outshooting Calvin Ward."

"I was just lucky in my shooting. Could either one of us won," Tom replied.

Shaking his head, Chess stood and looked at Tom. "It weren't luck. You shoot from the hip and hit what you shoot at. You got a knack. A knack that could get you challenged by some fool someday."

The word of the competition between Tom and Calvin spread like wildfire. Tom couldn't walk anywhere without someone calling out his name or offering to buy him a drink. He declined most offers of a drink. With Calvin Ward on the prowl, Tom figured he'd best stay sober.

Tom was stowing supplies he'd bought onto the mule when he saw the two Mexicans and Eva riding south. Her horse was being led and it looked like her hands were tied. Anger ran through Tom. A beautiful woman like Eva should be treated like a queen rather than an animal.

He watched them hurry south and knew he had no claim on her. It wasn't against the law to buy and sell brides in the west. The Arapahoe and other tribes had done it for hundreds of years. Even now, if Tom wanted a bride he could visit the Nez Perce lodges or the Flathead and make arrangement for a wife, for the price of a good horse.

"You don't keep a wife tied to a horse," Tom snorted.

Once again, Tom was feeling the pain of a loss. He brought the supplies back to the camp and looked around for Chess. His packs were neatly stowed in the teepee and a lukewarm pot of coffee sat next to the fire.

With his supplies put away, Tom poured a cup of the coffee. Swearing, he threw the coffee onto the ground and tossed the cup toward the teepee. He needed a real drink.

The company saloon was crowded with bearded mountain men. Leaning his elbows on the plank bar, Tom sipped on his fourth rye and made a decision. He would grow a beard and get an animal skin hat.

He turned to tell the drunken trapper next to him about his decision, when lights exploded in his head. Tom rolled to the dirt that made up the floor inside the saloon. Shaking his head to clear it, he looked up just in time to see the jubilant Calvin's low-cut boot coming at his head. Throwing himself aside, the boot clipped Tom's jaw, tearing a jagged cut.

The crowd stepped back, giving the men room. They were welcoming a good scrap. Tom felt rough hands grab him and pull him to his feet.

"Let's keep this a fair fight," the helpful man said.

Dazed, Tom looked at the vicious face of Calvin Ward. He had picked up Tom's drink from the bar and gulped it down. "Now, you young pup, I am going to give you a licking."

Tom saw Chess standing in the crowd, watching the fight. Other than watching his back in the case of unfair play, Tom couldn't expect any help from his partner. Each man stood on his own in a fight. Someone might pull a man off you before he beat you to death, but even that wasn't necessarily so.

Anger that had been building up with the loss of Eva and his dislike for Calvin Ward helped to clear Tom's head. Calvin closed in quickly to tackle Tom. He was expecting Tom to still be confused. That few seconds Calvin had taken to down the drink had probably saved him.

Tom lowered his head at the advancing man and met Calvin's nose with the top of his head. He could feel the cartilage crunch. In the same motion, he brought his right in with a wicked blow to Calvin's stomach. Shocked by Tom's response, Calvin stepped back, blood streaming from his broken nose. Gasping for air, Calvin grabbed a bottle from the bar and threw it at Tom.

Again, he charged, trusting his superior strength in a close contact fight. They exchanged blows, standing toe-to-toe. Finally, Tom stepped inside the big, right-hand roundhouse of Calvin and gave him several short punches to the body. Pushing him back, he followed with a left to Calvin's mouth.

A split lip that exposed ragged teeth added to the blood running down Calvin's dirty buckskin shirt. Still game, but not nearly as confident, Calvin came ahead. Tom stepped back to set himself and felt a man's leg in his way, no doubt a confederate of Calvin's.

Tom fell on his back, and gleefully Calvin closed in to leap on him. Tom raised his boots to push off the advance and missed Calvin's chest. His heels caught Calvin under the chin and snapped his head back.

Tom's opponent fell in an unconscious heap on the dirt floor. Tom struggled to get back to his feet. His nose was bleeding, along with his jaw. His right ear was ringing and he was having trouble seeing out of the right eye.

Chess stepped up to steady him. Tom would have figured he was looking into the proud face of a father, by the look on Chess.

"You gave that piece of dung a good whipping," he said.

"I think I need another drink, Chess."

Leaning on the bar, trying to catch his breath, Tom took a big taste of the rye. His mouth was instantly on fire as the alcohol found every cut. "Damn, that hurts," he said, swallowing the rye. "I am ready to go back to camp."

With his cuts cleaned up, Tom sat against the oak with his eyes closed, soaking up the late afternoon sun. Every move reminded him of the exchange of blows with Calvin Ward.

Chess nudged him and handed Tom a cup of hot coffee. "I was looking for you when I found you in the fight. Someone killed the old geezer."

Tom's eyes opened and he looked at Chess. "Did you say someone killed him?"

"Yep, cut him wide open and stole the money he got for the girl."

Tom sat straight up, feeling the pain shoot through his ribs. "When did this happen?"

Chess went back to the fire and added a couple more sticks. "It was sometime this morning. First, they suspected Indians, but the horses were left and the only thing taken was his money belt."

Tom had no doubt that there was blood on one of the Mexicans' daggers. It explained why they were hurrying south. He told Chess as much.

"Well, the men don't have to ride far south to be in Mexican territory. Ain't anyone down there that will care if there was a gringo killed."

"Gringo?"

Chess nodded. "That's what the Mexicans call us foreigners. I figure the men are headed for Santa Fe. The Arapahoe girl was mighty good-looking, so she will probably be sent to Mexico City to be kept as a servant or concubine for a wealthy landowner."

"Concubine? You know all kinds of big words, Chess."

"Well, a concubine is . . ."

Tom interrupted, "I think I can figure out what that is. Who went after them?" Tom asked.

"No one will bother," Chess said. "The old geezer wasn't liked much, and there is not much sense in wasting hard-earned supplies to hunt for trouble that isn't yours."

"I'm going to go and get her," Tom declared. "I will leave at first light."

It was just after two in the morning when Tom woke to the growling of the dog. It was lying next to him and he saw it disappear into the dark, toward the horses. There was a cry of pain, some shouting, braying of the mule, and a gunshot, followed by the yelp of the dog.

Tom grabbed his Colt and jumped to his feet. Ducking through the teepee flap, he ran bare foot in the direction of the commotion. He could hear Chess close behind. There was the sound of a galloping horse. The men stopped to listen. The echo of the horse disappeared and there was only the night sounds of frogs, crickets, and the heavy breathing of Tom and Chess.

"I think we had a horse stolen," Tom said as he slowly walked forward with his Colt level.

It was a moonless night and the men could see nothing. "I'll get a light," Chess volunteered, and he hurried back to the teepee.

Tom saw him pitch some kindling onto the coals to get a fire going. He then came walking with a candle, shielding the flame from the breeze.

The bay was gone. Tom and Chess figured that all their stock was the target, but the dog had intervened. The thieves had come from downwind, so the mule had not smelled them.

Tom's bare foot bumped something warm and furry lying on the ground. Kneeling down, he confirmed that it was the dog. Chess brought the candle over. It had been shot through the body and had died quickly.

Tom sank back and looked up at Chess. "It was a good dog."

In the morning light, Tom and Chess looked the area over. They found the tracks of one man. A bloody moccasin lay near the dog.

"Looks like the dog got one last lick in on the thief's leg," Chess said with satisfaction.

Tom dug a hole near the spot where the dog had died and buried it. A good dog deserves to be buried away from the buzzards and animals that would feed on it.

Tom returned to the camp and poured a cup of coffee. It was hot and strong, and always made him figure better.

"You think we should go after the horse thief?" Chess asked.

"I can't," Tom replied. "I have to go after Eva."

"You don't have a horse to ride," Chess reminded him.

"I got Ralph," Tom said, "and he will take me anywhere I need to go."

Tom was forced to delay another day caching his traps and other supplies he couldn't carry without a pack horse. He wanted to travel light and fast. It could be as much as 800 miles though mountains, desert, and hostile territory.

The Comanche and Apache would be a danger. There were Comancheros and the always dangerous Mexican Army. Water and food would be scarce. All these things were made clear to Tom by Chess.

"Maybe I will catch up to them before having to go too far south," Tom said with more confidence than he felt.

"I can't go with you, Tom," Chess said, "and I don't feel a bit good about it."

"I wouldn't expect you to go," Tom said sternly. "This is my fool's errand. I wouldn't think of endangering you on a trip like that."

"I heard there was some kind of fort or trading post near this side of the south pass," Tom added. "When I get Eva, I will be headed there to get married. You can leave me any word there in case my bay ever shows up."

"You are a forward thinker," Chess kidded him.

Tom felt better with a plan for the future. It gave him a feeling that things just might work out.

"I know a couple men that spent time in the direction you are headed," Chess said. "I can introduce you to them. They can let you know about the territory you are going into."

Tom spent the rest of the morning meeting with the men Chess recommended. He received sketched maps showing approximate locations of waterholes, and the most accessible passes through the mountains he would encounter. They also knew some towns that might be friendly to outsiders, in case he needed to replenish supplies.

Tom walked out of the trading tent and headed back to camp. Thanks to Chess' acquaintances, he had gained important information needed for the trip. He was carrying some last-minute items that would be helpful and was trying to think of anything he might have overlooked.

"Franklin, I am going to kill you!" The voice of Calvin Wood broke his thoughts.

Turning, he looked into the swollen face of the almost unrecognizable man.

"I am busy and don't have time for this, Calvin."

The men standing near the two moved back. Tom realized this was just like Calvin. Brace a man when his hands were full. Tom knew the loop was on his Colt. He was sure Calvin had also noticed that.

"Say hello to your dog when you get to the other side." Calvin's hand dropped for his gun.

The next few seconds were a blur to Tom. He dropped the supplies, and in a smooth motion flipped the loop of his Colt with his thumb. As he watched Calvin's gun come up, he was pulling his own. Fire spit from the barrel of Calvin's gun as Tom's cleared leather. He brought the gun level and fired.

Calvin jerked and fired again. Calvin's first shot had plowed dirt between the two men. His second shot went wide and ricocheted off the stone and clay ovens.

Tom shot a second time and watched Calvin's jaws work. His head was shaking back and forth. Whatever he was trying to say did not come out. He fell forward in a cloud of dust, firing once more into the ground.

In shock, Tom stood watching the man's blood spreading on the ground, soaking into the dust. The realization that he had just killed a man hit him. He put the Colt back into the holster so those who were watching wouldn't see it shake. His knees felt weak, and nausea gripped his stomach.

Chess was suddenly by his side, picking up his supplies. Tom doubted he could have stood back up had he stooped to retrieve them.

"You done good, Tom," Chess reassured him. "The man needed killing. This was the second time he blindsided you and he paid for it with his life."

Several men came up to Tom, congratulating him and vouching that it was a fair killing. Jim Bridger came out of the trading tent and quickly got the details on the fight. He walked up to Tom.

"The things I heard about your shooting are true," Jim said. "Calvin Ward wasn't worth the lead you used. I hear you are going after the Arapahoe woman. In my opinion, those Mexicans are in trouble."

"Thank you," Tom stammered.

"When you get back, contact me in St. Louis. I got some ventures planned and can use a good man."

With that said, Tom's mountain man hero, Jim Bridger, turned and walked back into the tent.

Tom pushed his way through the admiring crowd, turning down numerous offers of a drink. It made him think about the way men reacted to what had just happened. A cruel man's life had been ended. There had been more sympathy from these men when they found out that his dog was shot than he saw for Calvin Ward.

"I'll be leaving in the morning," Tom told Chess.

"What do you want to do with the stuff that isn't cached yet?"

"You keep it, Chess. I got no more time. I need to get out of here. Oh," Tom said, grinning, "The teepee is yours."

CHAPTER NINE

The morning sun found Tom already on the trail. He had previously checked out the area where the old geezer was killed. There was not much to be gained from the site. It had been trampled by those who had arrived before him.

He had ridden out and checked the trail the Mexicans had used. Their horses' tracks were committed to memory. Little else had been gained, but he knew their destination had to be Santa Fe. The men Chess had introduced to him provided a good description of the shortest and best routes to take.

It had been dark when Tom went out to saddle Ralph. The mule bit and kicked at him. It was enjoying the good life of grazing and sleeping. Being saddled told Ralph that there was work in his future.

Tom was sporting the start of a beard. He had put off getting the animal skin cap. He kept his flat-brimmed leather hat to help shed water and provide protection from the sun. The Hawken rifle was in its scabbard, and his Colt and skinning knife were on his belt. He had new leather pants and a shirt. In his saddlebags he had a pair of wool pants and a shirt. He carried a blanket that was cut to double as a poncho for warmth. His bedroll and poncho were wrapped in his rain slicker and tied to the back of his saddle.

He had plenty of gunpowder, precast lead and caps to use in the weapons. He had only a few days of prepared food, and after that Tom planned to hunt for meat. He had his mess kit, coffee, salt, cornmeal, dried beans, and jerky. He had roasted and crushed some of the coffee beans to save time on the trail. He had also brought some short, straight cigars, or cheroots, for smoking in the evening.

Ralph may have disagreed that he was traveling light with the gear he had. Tom missed having a pack animal to tote extra supplies, or to swap off for riding.

There had not been any rain, so Tom had no trouble following the trail. He had seen them leaving a couple of hours after daylight. It was apparent that they wanted to put distance between themselves and the rendezvous. Based on the distance they'd gone before Tom came across their first camp, it would have been well after dark before they had stopped.

Tom spent the night away from their camp. He wanted to check for sign in the morning and try to get a better picture of the men he was following. He sat near his small fire and stared at the heavens. Tom saw several shooting stars in the moonless sky, and wondered what made them fall out of the sky like that.

Sleep came slowly. Tom was anxious to look over the campsite and move on. He was several days behind the Mexicans. He wondered if Eva was being treated poorly. Their killing of the old geezer gave him just cause for going after them. He knew in his heart that Calvin Ward would not be the last man he would have to kill.

Morning found him huddled around the fire to keep warm. Tom waited for the sun to come up. He made the coffee weaker, having to conserve for the trip. He stared at a bright star on the eastern horizon. It was brighter than any of the others. He watched it with idle thoughts and hoped that one wouldn't fall out of the sky.

The Mexicans' camp gave Tom a better picture of his quarry. The men were careful and experienced in the outdoors. Eva was closely watched. One of the men had a "V" carved in the heel of his boots. The other might have a bad leg and stepped awkwardly. He noticed that Eva was wearing moccasins. A woman with soft feet was more valuable.

Care had been taken to put out their cook fire. He could see regimentation in the men, telling him that they may have been in the army at one time. Their trail was easy to follow. It appeared that once a little distance was put between them and the rendezvous, there was no fear of pursuit.

Tom spent the day studying the trail and watching the horizon. While he did not expect to find them yet, he might run into others who could give him trouble. He began to get the feeling that he was being followed. It was nothing he could see. Maybe dust on the back trail or a flash of light. It was so insignificant that he questioned if it was just nerves.

The Mexicans were keeping to lower ground. Care was taken not to skyline themselves. This was

Ute country and while the Ute were not currently on the warpath, it always made sense to keep your presence less noticeable. The three rested every two hours to conserve their horses. Their trail led from one waterhole to another, with little deviation.

Tom rode beyond their night camp before stopping on his second day. It was evident that the first day had taken its toll. A little extra rest was needed. Once again, Tom noticed the organization and well-chosen camp location.

His brown beard had grown to just over an inch-long. Looking at it in a still pond, he was surprised to see some gray streaks. He attributed it to the frontier living.

The trail was leading along the Green River Valley. Mountains rose on both sides. The area was beautiful. Tom hoped that he would have a chance to come back this way sometime. The men Chess had him meet with spoke of a mountain referred to as Pike's Peak. It had been first climbed by Edwin James, about 20 years ago. The Ute believed it was the beginning of the world. Tom hoped to see the great mountain.

The third day Eva had made a break for it. The Mexicans had just entered a narrow pass through two large boulders, forcing the party to ride single file. She was riding last. It appeared that she had spun her horse around, breaking loose from the man leading her horse. She had galloped west, making for a cliff overlooking the river.

Tom could only figure that she was going to jump the horse over the cliff and hope for the best. One of the Mexicans had caught up to her just before the cliff and tackled her. He could see where they had hit the loose sand. She had jumped up and ran again. By the length of her strides, her arms must have been loose to swing. The second Mexican had ridden up and grabbed her.

The horses had turned back toward their intended trail, stopping once to get Eva back onto her horse, no doubt tied again. She was then kept between the two Mexicans, one in front and the other in back.

As Tom rode back toward the trail, his heart was racing. He wondered what type of woman would risk her life to be free of capture. This would be a woman to live with in the mountains.

That night, Tom made dry camp. He kept his fire shielded by some boulders and made sure it was out after sundown. For two hours he laid on the top of one of the boulders and watched his back trail. At one point, he could have sworn that he saw the flicker of a fire. From his vantage point, he estimated that it could have been as far as five miles away.

The mule was grazing on some succulent grass and seemed content. Tom took a small drink out of his canteen and rolled up in his blankets. He thought about the person behind him. It could just be an innocent traveler using the same trail, or possibly a friend of Calvin Ward coming to settle a score. He thought back to the leg that had tripped him.

Tom woke to the smell of rain. Thunder heads were building in the west. The Mexicans had turned east, heading directly into a string of mountains. The elevation was over 5000 feet and the nights were cold. Tom realized that it was midsummer, but at these elevations one could face snow.

He watched the rain sweep across the valley behind him. Thunder was loud, with lightning bolts striking all around. Tom pulled up under an overhang of rock and watched the storm come. It was a blinding rain. Ralph snorted and kicked out each time the thunder clapped.

The Mexicans were heading over the mountains toward the high desert of the Colorado Territory. Tom figured that they were heading for the Cochetop Pass, which took its name from the Ute phrase 'pass of the buffalo'. A description and the name of the pass were on the sketches he had received.

The heavy rain lasted about two hours, turning the dry stream beds to roaring brown torrents of water. It slowed to a drizzle and Tom carefully turned Ralph along the trail east. Any sign of the three riders' trail was washed away. He knew little would be left in their campsites to confirm that he was still on their trail.

Tom was finally forced to stop when he reached a water-filled gorge. He watched the raging water, with tumbling logs and branches. Tonight would be a cold camp. With luck, the water would be down by morning and he could continue. Tom climbed to a low peak and looked at his back trail. He pulled his poncho and slicker tighter. The wind in the mountains was cold and he was a little damp from the rain.

He was just about dozing when he caught sight of a fire. Tom watched it for over a half hour. This confirmed his fear. He was being followed. Nobody would follow the trail he was on unless it was to pursue him.

Tom had learned much from Two Buffalo about tracking. He would reverse this knowledge and make his trail invisible. He felt a degree of comfort confirming that he was being followed. His progress would be slower, but he must now take action.

The sun was bright and the water in the gorge was just a trickle in the morning. Tom felt good. He had made a small fire for coffee and boiled some beans with pieces of jerky. It had been fine dining after eating out of the saddlebag the past couple days.

Tom's mission had become threefold. He had to find Eva and evade his pursuer. While doing this, he would have to hunt for food.

Tom patted Ralph on the nose. "No problem."

The tracks he was following were gone. Travel options for the Mexicans were few. He knew that they were trying to get to the high desert and then head south to Santa Fe. Tom's only worry was getting into a dead-end valley and having to backtrack. Studying the sketches, he had a high degree of confidence that he could stay clear of these.

Tom rode on rocky ledge whenever possible or would keep Ralph in the middle of streams. He remained vigilant and felt he was making good progress. Tom hoped that the problems he was encountering would also slow the Mexicans down.

For three days, he worked hard at making his trail disappear. Any fires were buried and smoothed over. Only loose wood was used, no breaking branches. He came across a small deer feeding in a glen. It was early afternoon when he shot it, but Tom waited to gut and skin it until he stopped for nightfall.

He took care to bury the parts he could not use by caving in a sandy bank. The sign of a caved bank he could not hide, but it would prevent high-flying buzzards from leading anyone following him to his trail.

In any other circumstance, Tom would have been in his glory. The magnificence of the jutting, rocky points surrounded by pines was breathtaking. Each valley connecting to another brought inexplicable beauty. Mountain flowers like the blue columbine covered the valley floors. Elk, deer, and mountain sheep could be seen daily. Rabbits were plentiful and Tom would dispatch one for supper with his Colt.

Ralph was good company. Tom talked to him about his dreams and goals. The mule's ears would cock back and forth, listening to the rider.

Tom did not see any more fire behind him when he watched at night. He figured that the follower had been evaded. A more current worry was unshod pony tracks that he came across. He doubted the Ute would approve of a trapper riding through on a mule.

Tom felt a twinge of regret when he reached the high desert plains. He could still enjoy the mountains to his west, but now it was from afar. It reminded him of his first trip to see them with Gus and Hector.

Tom came upon the Mexicans' trail almost by accident. He was looking for some supper and was tracking a deer into the foothills. He saw some shod horse tracks. He followed them a short distance and was sure they were made by his quarry. If he had not chased the deer tracks, he would have missed them to the east. Days might have been lost before he'd have crossed them again.

It was less than a half-hour from sunset when Tom finally made camp. He was tired from the long ride and the mule required more encouragement to keep moving, but Tom hated to stop. The tracks he was following were less than three days-old. He was making good time.

Tom's routine was unchanged. Before bedding down, he watched his back trail for an hour. Far to the east he caught sight of a fire, maybe hunters or Cheyenne. There was nothing behind him. The next morning, he was riding at first light.

Ralph seemed to like several of the high desert plants. He was chewing most of the time they rode. Tom did not mind, because there was little enough time to graze in the evening. He worried some about the weight Ralph seemed to have lost.

Tom rode into a grove of aspen and looked out over the rolling hills when he saw some buzzards circling something ahead. He swung down from the mule and loosened the cinch. Sitting on a rock ledge, Tom ate some cold rabbit and drank a little water. He missed having biscuits.

He continued to watch the buzzards. Originally, there had been a half-dozen and now he could only see two. With his noon meal done, he tightened the cinch and swung back onto the mule.

Ralph was ready to go. Tom could see a thin line of trees that went out onto the desert plain. That meant a stream or river. They had been riding dry most of the day and the mule smelled the water.

When Tom rode over the rise, the first thing he saw was a grove of cottonwood. In the cottonwood branches there sat several buzzards. He continued to ride forward. All of a sudden, Ralph turned his head and brayed.

Tom searched the grove for anything that was amiss. He finally saw several buzzards walking around under the trees. Apparently, there was something that wasn't quite ready to be eaten. Tom turned Ralph away from the buzzards and urged him toward the water.

He swung down near the stream and watered the mule. Tom knelt upstream and drank some of the cold, clear water. He tied the mule to some low branches that would allow close grazing. Taking the Hawken rifle, Tom walked toward the cottonwoods to see what interested the buzzards.

He stopped abruptly. Lying on the ground were the bloated bodies of two men. The bodies were positioned like they had been crawling to get away while someone shot them repeatedly. There were flies and ants crawling over them.

Tom sat on his heels and stared at the men. He could see the "V" carved in the boots of one. These were the men who had bought Eva. Their cook pots were still on the now cold fire. Bed rolls had been spread out and remained untouched. He could see where the horses had been picketed.

Fear clutched his stomach. What had become of Eva? There wasn't any evidence that anyone else had been killed. A new group of people far worse than the Mexicans now had her. Tom began to read the sign.

There were tracks of a dozen horses. Slow examination of the sight told a gruesome story. The Mexicans had been preparing supper when the riders came up. The incoming riders had spread out to surround the men and Eva. Tom found where the two Mexicans had kneeled. The shots had come from behind, knocking them forward.

The shots were not killing shots. The objective had been not to kill the men quickly. They were allowed to crawl a distance while wounding shots were inflicted. There were also near-misses.

The men crawled about 20 feet before being wounded too severely to continue. The riders had moved away and dismounted. It was presumably in the area Eva had been taken. From this point the cold-blooded killers had watched as the two men bled out and died.

There were several horse droppings at this location, confirming that it might have taken an hour or more before the men expired.

Was it justice? These men in front of him had killed the old geezer in cold blood. The money given for Eva had been taken back. Tom shook his head. "You poor bastards may have deserved dying, but not like this."

Tom had nothing to dig graves with. He looked at the large, black buzzards sitting in the cottonwood limbs, waiting for the meal below. The loud buzzing of flies was a constant reminder of the bodies.

Using the men's blankets, he wrapped them. Dragging the bodies, he dumped them into a depression made by a windfall. Brush and limbs were piled over the two men. Tom then lit the pile. Once the fire burned out, there would not be much left of the two men. This the buzzards could have.

The mule was happy to see Tom return. Slipping the Hawken back into the scabbard, Tom checked the cinch and swung into the saddle. The sobering realization was that his quest had now changed.

The men who had Eva now might also choose to sell her. A beautiful woman was valuable in Mexico. Tom also knew that the men might just decide to use and abuse her, eventually leaving her lifeless body to the flies and buzzards.

The carnage he had just witnessed had happened less than two days ago. That gave Tom some hope of catching up with them. He had closed in from a four-day lead to less than two. The difference was that now he would be facing a large number of men who enjoyed killing.

There were still four hours before the sun went down. Tom moved out to follow the riders. He would have to ride with care. On the other side of the stream, he found the tracks of a two-wheel cart. Tom guessed that Eva had been put into it.

Tom rode between large boulders that were scattered along the foothills of the mountains. The breeze rustled the aspen leaves. Groups of dark green pines and other evergreens stood out in the hills.

It was looking like rain again. Dark clouds were building over the mountains. The water would be welcome in the dry, high desert plains. Little rain fell during the summer months. Tom could see the riders' tracks below on the plain. He felt less exposed riding in the tree and boulder-covered hills.

Suddenly, four men came out of the trees, riding fast down the hillside. Their sombreros were hanging on their backs and the silver-trimmed powder horns slapping against homespun shirts. Holding their guns in the air, they spurred the horses at Tom.

Tom wheeled the mule as he drew his Colt. Then everything went black. He could hear a voice. It sounded like Isaac. Tom tried to call to his brother. As the men continued to shoot, Tom felt nothing.

CHAPTER TEN

Eva sat in the two-wheel cart, praying that the men would forget her. It seemed like ages ago when the old man Samuel had traded the rifle for her. It was hard to understand why her father would have done that. The truth was that he had too many daughters and too few guns.

The Arapahoe were a proud tribe, but too much fighting had left her father weak. With the rifle, buffalo could be hunted and enemies could be killed.

Eva could hear the laughter of the men riding alongside the cart. They were dirty men with many guns and horses. The large hats and loose-fitting clothing made them seem bigger than they were.

Eva had met a Methodist circuit rider when she was young. His goal had been to covert the Indians to Christianity. He had given her the name Eva. She had learned some English from him, but no Spanish. The men who now held her spoke Spanish. They had crowded around her after shooting the two men who had purchased her.

With evil smiles, they had poked and touched her, tearing at her gingham dress. A fat, cruel man they called jefe had shouted at them, making them leave her alone. He had said the word concubina when he pointed at her.

There had been disappointment on the men's faces, which only made them look more dangerous.

Eva thought back to the past few months. Samuel had only been interested in having her cook and take care of him. He had hit her, but never on the face. She'd accepted the fact that Samuel was to be obeyed and had done her best to anticipate his needs. Had he demanded, she would have laid with him at night, but no request had come.

Eva could not understand him tying her hands. Did he fear she would hurt him? If she had hurt him or even left him, she would have had no place to go. Her people would not have understood if Eva had returned alone.

One day, Samuel had come out of a trading post and held up a chain with a ring on the end. This he had put around her ankle, and she was forced to wear it day and night. When he would go away, the loose end of the chain was fastened to the wagon.

Eva remembered the time last winter when she'd sat with the chain on and wearing a buffalo robe. A tall man had walked by and glanced at her. Eva had pretended not to notice him, but in her heart, she wondered why her father couldn't have found a man like him to trade with.

She had worked hard for Samuel through the winter. When he would go hunting, the chain would be secured near enough to the fireplace so she could keep it burning.

Eva had begged him not to chain her, promising she would not leave. Samuel had snorted, "You are my little investment. A man doesn't take chances with an investment."

The word investment was foreign to Eva. Maybe it meant not to be trusted, because that is the way he had treated her.

When traveling to the rendezvous, he had begun to tie her wrists again. Often, she had both the leg chain and bound wrists. Samuel's behavior had been hard to understand.

Once at the rendezvous, he had taken her to the river and made her bathe and wash her hair. He had not seemed to care how many men saw her naked or made lewd comments. He had brought out a deerskin dress for her to wear.

He had removed the chain from her leg and made her sit on a log near the fire. Samuel had warned her, "If you run, I will find you and kill you."

Why he had said these things, Eva did not know. She had been his, and there was no place for her to run to.

Several men had come by to talk with Samuel. They would stand near the wagon while she sat out of earshot on the log. She could see them argue back and forth, and then the men would leave.

One day, two men who spoke a language that Eva did not understand had come to the wagon. They had talked with Samuel for some time. At one point, Samuel had called her over and made her remove her dress. It was humiliating and confused Eva. She'd been glad when they had left.

The following morning, the sun was barely up when Samuel had taken her near a crowd of men who were listening to music. Eva saw the two men again and felt scared. Samuel had pushed her closer to them and talked of money. That was when a man had walked up and said something very odd.

He had talked about her being spoken for and that she couldn't be sold. While she had wondered about the stranger's statement, one of the two men had hit him in the back of the head and then all three began to punch him.

Samuel had grabbed her and led her back to the wagon. He'd then put the chain back on her ankle. It had slowly sunk into Eva's mind that Samuel was trying to sell or trade her. It had not made sense. He did not need another gun. He'd had enough horses. It could only be that she did not make him happy.

The two men had come back with a dress made of cloth. They'd spoken with Samuel, then smiling had handed him the dress. When they'd left, Samuel had walked over to her.

He had handed her the dress. "Put this here dress on and bring me the deerskin outfit. I can get a couple dollars for it."

She had sat on the log with the new dress. It had felt flimsy and thin. She hadn't felt properly covered in it.

Suddenly, the tall man had walked into camp and passed in front of her. He had spoken briefly with

Samuel. From the corner of her eye, Eva had watched his face sadden. He had then walked behind her and away. Maybe Samuel would trade her to the tall man. Eva knew better by the look on his face.

The men whom Samuel called Mexicans had given money for her. She knew this because Samuel had shown her the money belt and, once again, called her an investment that paid off. He had chained her to the wagon and walked away with a spring in his step, heading for the saloon.

Turning for a moment, he had warned her, "Don't you be getting that new dress dirty. The Mexicans wouldn't like that."

Samuel had come back late and was drunk. He had looked at her and laughed. Soon, he'd been snoring under the wagon. He had forgotten her, chained. It had been a long night.

The two Mexicans had come the next morning, one carrying a pair of moccasins to put on her feet. He had tied her wrists and then lifted her onto a horse. She had struggled to arrange the dress.

One of the men had stayed and talked with Samuel while the other had mounted his horse and led hers past the trading tent. Soon, his friend had caught up and they quickly rode south, leading her horse.

Eva had caught a glimpse of the tall man loading supplies onto a mule. She would never see him again. The Mexicans had not adjusted her stirrups, and Eva had struggled to stay on the horse as they'd left the rendezvous.

While riding south, Eva had decided that she would escape. Maybe she could get back to the rendezvous and ask the tall man to help her.

The first day had been the longest ride. After that, the men had seemed more relaxed. They would laugh and talk, looking at her and pointing. The fatter one, who had led her horse from Samuel's camp, was named Ricco. He had a quick smile. The other was Juan. Juan was lean and had a cruel face.

Eva had watched for the chance to get away. One day, riding along a plateau, she had seen where the river wound near the edge. She had decided that if she could leap into the river, she could swim to freedom.

The chance had come when they'd went through some narrow rocks. The bonds on her wrists were loosened and it was time.

Eva had wheeled her horse and kicked as hard as she could to make it run. She could hear the men close behind. Eva had known that she would have to leap the horse over the cliff. Ricco had caught up and knocked her from the horse.

Regaining her feet, Eva had continued to run for the cliff. Juan had galloped up and grabbed her hair, lifting her across his saddle. That night, the men had shouted and threatened her. Eva was resigned. She had tried, and it was doubtful that another chance would come.

The trip over the mountains had been cold. Eva had been given a wool poncho to wear. When it rained, the Mexicans had slipped a slicker over her head. She did not have a hat and the water had run down her hair, soaking her under the slicker.

Eva was sitting, tied near the stream, when the bad men had come. There were many, and the sound of their horses and the shouting had been terrifying. She had crouched behind a tree, shaking with fear.

Ricco and Juan had stood with rifles and looked around at the men surrounding them.

Outnumbered, Ricco and Juan had set their rifles onto the ground. The men had forced them to kneel and pray. Eva had hoped they would go away. Suddenly, there had been a gunshot and Ricco twisted and fell. Another shot had knocked Juan down. As the two wounded men crawled, the riders kept shooting at them and laughing. Soon Ricco and Juan had been unable to crawl.

Eva was horrified and had begun to run. The men quickly caught her. They then stood and watched as Ricco and Juan had moaned and begged for help. The ground around them was covered with blood. It had seemed like an eternity before the two men lay still.

The cart hit a rock and jolted Eva back to the present. She fell heavily against the side. She looked for something to cut her bonds. Her feet were numb from the leather ties. Eva's wrists were chafed and bleeding.

The cart had food items, pots, and bedding. Pulling a pot over, she rubbed the wrist bonds against the edge. It was too dull, and did nothing but cause more abrasion of her wrists. The canvas over the cart prevented any breeze from getting into the confined space. Exhausted from her ordeal, hot and thirsty, Eva finally slipped into semi-conscious sleep.

She woke to coolness. The jarring of the cart had stopped. The back hatch opened and she felt rough hands drag her out. The man called jefe began to shout at the men again. He pointed at the bloody wrists and swollen feet. It was obvious that Jefe did not want Eva injured by her bonds.

Eva was dragged towards a large cave. They had untied her, but she was light-headed and any pressure on her feet felt like thousands of needles pricking her. Two strap iron cages sat in the back of the cave. The big door of one was opened and she was pushed in. Eva fell among the other prisoners. Looking up, she saw several Mexican and Indian women. She gratefully accepted the water offered by one. Eva sat in the iron cage, unaware of the struggle happening several miles back on their trail.

Tom was running from something. He tried to hurry, but his legs wouldn't move. He could hear others telling him to come, but he couldn't. He became aware of something cool touching his forehead. Slowly, he opened his eyes. It was dark and hazy. There was the smell of someone near him.

Shouting, he tried to roll to safety and the world began to spin. He was falling into darkness. He braced himself, expecting to hit the bottom, which would not come.

Two Buffalo looked at his friend as he struggled and uttered unintelligible words. Sadness was heavy in his heart. His friend was in a battle with the devil, and all Two Buffalo could do was sit by and watch.

It had been three days since he had found Tom. That had been one day after finding the charred remains of two men. Much had happened at the camp. There were many tracks and much blood. A brief shower had erased the complete story, but enough had remained to tell him that vicious acts had happened.

Two Buffalo had returned to his village after Tom left for the rendezvous. He had been welcomed with shouts and smiles. Everyone had been impressed with the large cougar hide and very much so with the strong medicine necklace. The necklace had claws and teeth of the great silver bear. These were separated by colored stones and pieces of copper. A golden nugget the size of a prairie chicken egg hung in the bottom center.

Other elders had taken over the council. He had seen distrust, even envy, in their eyes. At times they had met without letting him know. The elders were angry. Two Buffalo had left to die and then come back with powerful things. He had cheated the Great Spirit, or had he been blessed by it. Either way, they did not intend to share in the leadership of the tribe.

Two Buffalo had decided that he no longer belonged or had the respect of the tribe leaders. It was time to go. Trading the cougar skin for a paint horse and long rifle, he had left to find a true friend, Tom Franklin. He had known of the rendezvous at the Green River. When he'd arrived at the Green River, there had been much talk of the man Tom Franklin, but Tom had left to rescue an Arapahoe woman.

Chess had told him of the night Tom's bay had been stolen and the dog shot. This had angered Two Buffalo. While the dog had often growled at him, it had been a good dog. Chess had told him about the two Mexicans taking the Arapahoe woman and killing the old geezer. When sorting out the geezer's gear, it had been discovered that his name was Samuel.

Early the next morning, Two Buffalo had ridden out on the trail of Tom. The mule stepped heavily and it had been easy to follow the tracks. His paint had moved out readily. It was shod and probably had been stolen from white men.

The trail had been easy to follow, until the great rain. Two Buffalo had lost it, and for miles at a time had only occasionally picked up a partial track, or a dropping from Ralph. It did not make sense that Tom had started hiding his trail. He was the one hunting and not the hunted.

After finding the charred bodies, the trail had been easy to see. The first thing Two Buffalo had found was the mule. He'd noticed Ralph grazing just below some lodge pole pines. It had taken an hour to coax the leery animal close enough to grab the reins. Then it had been all Two Buffalo could do to prevent being kicked or bitten. Finally, the saddle had slipped under Ralph's belly and it seemed that the mule had realized that it needed help.

The Hawken rifle had slid out of the scabbard. Two Buffalo had pulled the cinch loose and let the saddle and gear fall to the ground. Securely tying the mule to some low branches, he had returned to collect the gear.

Ralph had been wandering for a while, and to follow the tracks would have taken some time. Two Buffalo had scanned the horizon, looking for any sign of where Tom might be. He had seen some black birds riding the updraft south of his location.

Saddling Ralph back up and loading the gear, he had gotten his paint and had ridden to investigate.

He'd found Tom lying face down. His head had been covered with dried blood and several other areas of his body had shown signs of bullet wounds.

Two Buffalo could see where riders had approached. He surmised that Ralph had run when Tom was shot.

The riders had sat on their horses briefly and then had galloped south, following a two-wheel cart trail. Two Buffalo had been sure Tom was dead. He'd knelt to roll his friend over and had heard a soft moan.

That had been three days ago, and Two Buffalo used all his years of experience making poultices to treat Tom. His friend had lost a lot of blood. The wound on his head looked ugly, but in reality the bullet had hit a side buckle on Tom's hat. Once fragmented, the bullet had torn a wide path across the side of his head.

The blood and skin from this had no doubt convinced the riders that his brains were falling out. The other shots had been confirmation shots, making sure the man was dead. All five were flesh wounds on his legs and sides.

Two Buffalo had been patiently waiting for his good friend to slip into the spirit world so he could give him a proper burial. In the last day, Tom had been running a fever and was delirious much of the time. Two Buffalo had boiled some aspen bark and tried to get Tom to drink some. It would help the fever.

Darkness came on. Two Buffalo had built a small fire and taken care of the animals. Ralph was getting used to him, but would still bite or kick if given a chance. He sat near the fire dozing after putting a damp cloth on Tom's forehead.

"Are we dead?" A raspy voice startled Two Buffalo.

He looked into the deathly pale face of his friend. Tom stared intently at him.

"We are not dead," Two Buffalo answered. "But you, my friend, have been close."

Tom coughed hoarsely. He lay back and looked at the night sky. Two Buffalo came and offered him something to drink. Tom swallowed the bitter brew.

"That is awful," he said, choking on the liquid.

"It will keep the fever away. It comes from the bark of the aspen," Two Buffalo explained.

Tom lay quietly for a moment. It should be colder. He moved his arm out of the blankets and felt the grass-covered dirt. "What happened to the snow?"

Two Buffalo gave a worried look to his friend. "It is now summer. You were searching for an Arapahoe woman. You were shot by Comancheros."

Tom had fallen back to sleep. His forehead was covered with beads of sweat. Two Buffalo sat back and grunted, "Good, the fever has broken."

For the next two days, Tom awoke for short periods. Quickly tiring, he'd fall back asleep. Each time he had been more aware of where he was and had been able to remember what Two Buffalo had told him.

It was just getting light and Two Buffalo was returning with an armload of wood. He found Tom sitting up on his blankets. The color had come back to his cheeks and he had a good appetite.

"I will have breakfast ready soon. The coffee is ready. I'll pour you a cup," Two Buffalo said.

"I need to go after Eva. By now they are days away," Tom said, with urgency in his voice.

157

"And when you get there, they will kill you," Two Buffalo said flatly. "You are too weak to fight. A blow to the head would be your end."

Tom's wounds were healing quickly, thanks to the poultice Two Buffalo applied. His skull had taken a severe blow and care had to be taken. Tom was dizzy less frequently, and was able to move around the camp. He still tired quickly and the ache in his head remained. Any exertion would make the side of his head throb with his heartbeat.

Tom's gear was intact, thanks to the mule running away when he was shot. His Colt had flown from his hand and was overlooked by the attackers.

"You learned well," Two Buffalo said.

"What did I learn?" Tom questioned.

"You can read sign of others and hide your trail as good as any. When following you, I was proud of what I was seeing."

"I sure missed the men that shot me," Tom stated.

"They had the high ground and were lucky. The men were trying to catch up to the two-wheel cart. They ran across you by accident. Being the type of men they were, you were shot for fun."

Two Buffalo added wood to the fire. "Tomorrow, we will follow the cart and find your woman Eva. Now, I will go and bring back some fresh meat for supper."

CHAPTER ELEVEN

Feeling tired, Tom decided to rest until Two Buffalo returned with supper. He slept like the dead. For years Tom had slept light, the slightest sound waking him. Since the head wound, he would fall into a deep sleep. Two Buffalo promised that with time Tom would again be a light sleeper. The deep sleep was a healing sleep.

The men were right on top of Tom before he woke. Sitting on their horses only feet away were the men who had attacked him.

"Look here, amigos, this gringo is hard to kill. Jefe sends us back to find the mule and instead we find the one we have already killed," the lean, pock-faced Comanchero chortled.

The man to his left smiled broadly, showing the missing front teeth. His fat stomach shook as he laughed and he said, "We will not make the mistake of leaving him alive again, amigo."

The four men covered Tom on three sides, and with great pleasure drew their well-worn cap and ball revolvers.

Tom froze for a moment, confused at what he was seeing. An arrow appeared in the chest of the pock-faced man. While he slid from his horse, fighting for breath, the other three wheeled their horses. A second arrow hit one of the men low in the back. He hunched over, grabbing the mane of his horse.

By this time, Tom had slid his Colt from under his saddle. Lying on his side, he fired at the portly man, hitting him high in the back, a killing shot. The fourth man spurred his horse, quickly putting distance between himself and Tom.

Tom's Hawken rifle was lying loaded next to his blankets. He picked up the Hawken and lay on his stomach with the rifle to his shoulder. Taking careful aim, he squeezed the aft trigger and then touched off the front trigger.

The rifle recoiled, sending a .50 caliber bullet through the fleeing Comanchero and into the neck of his horse. Tom did not see the man and horse collapse in a heap. He was curled up on the ground with his eyes shut, waiting for the pain in his head to subside.

The shock of the recoil and the noise of the rifle going off next to his head sent waves of agony through him. He felt a hand on his shoulder.

"Are you okay, Tom?" It was the anxious voice of Two Buffalo.

"My head, when I shoot the rifle it hurts my head," he groaned.

Three of the Comancheros lay dead along with one of their horses. One man had disappeared, carrying Two Buffalo's arrow. The other horses had followed the wounded man.

"I didn't hear them," Tom said. "I fell asleep and they rode right up to me!"

Two Buffalo assured Tom that he would again be a light sleeper in the future.

"I just hope I am not dead before that happens," Tom replied.

While Two Buffalo used the paint to drag the dead Comancheros away from their camp Tom sat with his head pounding. Once it was a dull ache, he put some wood onto the cold ashes and got the fire going. Two Buffalo had brought back two rabbits and a prairie chicken for their evening meal.

The next sunrise found the two men in the saddle, following the Comancheros. Tom figured if the men had ridden back to their main camp after shooting him, and then were sent back for the mule, the main camp couldn't be over four days travel away. With luck, they would find Eva there.

While Tom and Two Buffalo were working out the Comancheros' trail, Eva sat in the cool, dark cave leaning against the rough strap-iron bars. Someone had put a lot of work into the eight by ten cages. The one Eva was in held the young and middle-aged women. They were fed once a day. A bucket used as a toilet was emptied by two of the older women each morning. Another bucket with drinking water sat on the other side of the cage.

The other cage held young and middle-aged men. Some of the men showed signs of having been beaten. No doubt the beatings had happened when being captured or after attempts to escape. The body of one man who had been caught trying to escape hung in the entrance of the cave as a reminder to the others.

One night, the Comancheros were drinking heavily and the sound of the drunken men came closer. Two men came in and opened the cage door. One of the middle-aged women was ordered to come with them. Her screams were heard late into the night.

Whether she lived or died, Eva did not know. The woman was not seen again. The cruelty of the men who held them captive was terrifying. Eva had heard stories of such atrocities being done by Arapahoe warriors when they captured enemies. She had never been so close to it.

Eva awoke one morning, hearing men shouting and entering the cave. She was sure they were about to die. "So be it," she said under her breath. "I am ready."

The cages were opened and the prisoners were lined up. Each had their hands bound with lengths of hemp rope. The rough rope cut into Eva's wrists. They were led from the cave. The morning sun was bright and made it difficult to see.

There were two carts loaded and hitched to oxen. The ends of the captives' ropes were tied to the back of one of the two-wheel carts. Eva looked around the canyon where they had been kept. The steep sides had lookouts posted around the perimeter. The dust-covered canyon floor had garbage from the many meals scattered about. She could see the tumbleweed and wild grass on the desert plain at the canyon opening.

Jefe assembled his men, shouting orders in Spanish. He pointed to Eva and two men grabbed her, tossing her into one cart. The hemp rope was replaced with leather string, carefully tied so that it wasn't too tight. She had little room. A canteen of water was left near her.

The back was closed and the canvas was pulled over the top. The cart lurched forward. Looking through the crack on the side boards, she saw three horses standing to the side. Two of them had blood on them. One had a significant amount, telling her that whoever had ridden that horse had bled for some time. Eva sat in the stifling heat of the cart unaware that anyone was following, searching for her.

Two Buffalo rode down from a hill side and joined Tom. "Something is lying on the plain ahead."

Riding closer revealed the body of the man Two Buffalo had hit low in the back with an arrow. He had lasted a day and a half before falling from the horse. The men could see where wolves had gotten to him. Others would return tonight, and soon very little would be left of the man.

Two Buffalo did not slow as he rode past the body. "We do not have time to take care of the likes of him. Let the wilds take care of it," he told Tom.

As they rode, Tom was feeling stronger, rather than weaker. He was confident that when they caught the other Comancheros he would be ready. He thought back to the killing of the four men. He felt no guilt or remorse. He had none of the feelings he'd had with Calvin. It wasn't a realization that made him feel good.

Tom and Two Buffalo were riding in the tree line of the foothills for cover. Suddenly, Tom glimpsed a flash of light ahead of them. Two Buffalo was already off the paint before Tom could say anything, tying his horse to a small maple.

"I will go ahead. You save your strength for the fight. It will be dark in three hours. If we attack, it will be after dark." With that, Two Buffalo disappeared into the trees.

Tom swung off Ralph. He chewed on some cold rabbit and sipped water from the canteen. Sitting on a windfall, Tom checked the Hawken load, then the Colt. He took an extra revolver from his saddle bag that he'd taken from one of the dead Comancheros. Checking it closely to make sure the gun was ready, he put it into his belt.

Tom made up his mind that he would not fire the Hawken rifle from the shoulder unless absolutely necessary. While his head felt much better, he didn't want to take a chance on being blinded with pain.

While waiting for Two Buffalo, Tom dozed on and off. His friend had told him rest was important, but the search for Eva should be his. Therefore, he should be taking the risks, not his friend.

Tom looked up when the paint whinnied. Glancing at the animals he noticed that Ralph was busy grazing while the paint stared expectantly toward the direction in which Two Buffalo had gone. Tom sat with his hand on the Colt, just in case it was someone else coming out of the trees. Soon, he saw the familiar shape of his friend.

Quickly, Two Buffalo drew the layout in the dirt. "They are in a canyon with 30-foot sides. I counted three guards on the walls. Two are at the front, one in the back. The canyon opening is on the east side. I could hear men in the canyon. It was the sound of men that are drinking."

Tom looked at the diagram. "Can we get to the men on top?"

"We come in from the back. The rear guard can be taken first. We will then need to split up to get the front guards. I will make the sound of a night dove. That will be the signal to take him down. From that point, we can get to the canyon floor without much trouble. We have to try and get close and take them by surprise. It is our only chance against so many men."

Tom was impressed with Two Buffalo's strategy. He must have been a formidable enemy years ago.

Two Buffalo looked Tom straight in the eye. "We will have to kill the guards on the wall. We can't take a chance leaving them unconscious. Can you kill with a knife?"

"I can do what is necessary," Tom replied.

Satisfied, Two Buffalo showed Tom the best way to hold and stab an opponent. "This way the man goes down quietly, unable to cry out."

Their horse and mule were brought as close as possible to the Comancheros' camp, just in case they needed to get away. There was a half-moon working against them. Stealth would be critical. The two men worked their way along the back of the canyon wall. Tom saw the guard sitting on a boulder, watching his fellow Comancheros drinking below.

Two Buffalo held his hand up for Tom to wait. He moved ahead like a ghost. Tom lost sight of him and waited. His stomach was tight. The tension of the night made his head throb. Tom prayed that he would be able to hold his end up.

The guard sitting on the rock was there one moment and then gone. Other than the slight sound of cloth dragging over stone, there was nothing. It was time to go after his man.

Tom moved along the canyon wall, taking advantage of cover provided. A cloud drifted over the moon and Tom made good time crossing an open area, getting closer to his objective.

Pausing a moment, Tom double-checked his knife. He knew the blade was razor-sharp, but checking helped his nerves. Slowly, he was able to make out the silhouette of his targeted guard. Tom hid less than 10 paces from the man.

It seemed like an eternity while he waited. Tom was sure the man would hear his pounding heart. Finally, another cloud covered the moon, and a second later he heard the sound of a dove.

Closing the distance between himself and the guard, Tom moved in with his knife low. As he reached the guard, the man turned and looked at him. His mouth opened to shout as Tom's hand clamped over it. Tom thrust the knife up and under the man's ribcage. He could feel the man twist and try and hit him with the gun. He tried to bite Tom's hand. The struggles weakened and rifle slipped from the man's grip and fell to the rocks.

Tom let the man drop and grabbed his hat. He then stood holding the man's rifle, and wearing his hat just in case anyone looked up at the sound. It was not necessary. Those below were too busy drinking.

He casually walked further on the ledge, out of sight of anyone below. Tossing the hat aside, Tom donned his own and worked his way to the canyon floor. He waited until another cloud passed and walked briskly across the opening to meet Two Buffalo.

There were a half-dozen Comancheros sitting around the fire pit, passing a bottle. The two spent a few moments searching out any men away from the fire. Finally concluding that the party around the fire was all that was visible in the canyon, they moved quietly toward the men.

"Don't move or we will shoot you!" Tom commanded. He held two revolvers leveled at the men. The Hawken was slung over his shoulder with a leather strap.

Two Buffalo stood on Tom's left, holding his long rifle and had a gun in his belt. One of the Comancheros grabbed for a gun and Two Buffalo put a ball from the long rifle through his shoulder, knocking the man to the ground. The other five men froze in place. The tension of the moment made Tom's heart pound and his legs shake.

While Two Buffalo held his cap and ball handgun on the men, Tom moved quickly toward the cave. The adrenalin made him feel light-headed as he moved along the stone wall. The cave was as still as a tomb. There was a lit lantern next to the opening. Carefully removing it from the peg, he entered the cave, staying close to the wall. The light fell on the empty cages. His hopes were dashed on finding Eva in the canyon. He next checked the second cave.

Flame from a gun stabbed out from the dark recess. Tom dropped the lantern and returned fire at the flash. Pressing against the cool wall, Tom waited. He was thankful that the lantern went out when dropped.

If Tom moved away from the wall, he would be back-lighted by the moon. The inside of the cave was black as pitch. Tom would have to use sound to locate the man. There was a scrape of a boot on the stone floor.

In a, low clear, voice Tom told the person inside, "In a moment I will begin firing in the cave. With luck, you may survive the ricocheting bullets."

Again, he heard movement. Something was bumped and fell over. Tom fired at the sound and flattened himself against the wall.

"Por favor, no disparen," the man said in Spanish.

Tom held himself back, not moving. He could hear the slow footsteps coming out of the cave.

"Hurry up and get out here," Tom ordered.

He glimpsed the man's shadow and saw moonlight reflect off something waist-high.

The man took a chance and shot at Tom. The bullet sprayed stinging granite into Tom's face. Instinctively, Tom fired at the shadow. There was a grunt and the sound of something falling to the floor.

Tom moved back, blinking to clear his eyes. He waited a moment and slowly made out the form of the man lying on the cave floor. Retrieving the lantern,

Tom went back to the firepit and relit the wick. Returning to the cave, he carefully looked to make sure there were no other Comancheros or prisoners.

A shove with his toe told him that the man on the floor was dead. Tom looked at the impressive amount of supplies. He saw kegs of gunpowder and was thankful that one of his shots hadn't hit them. Convinced that the cave had no one else hiding inside it, Tom returned to the fire.

"Where are the people that were in the cages?" he demanded.

The men looked at him with blank faces. None of the Comancheros spoke English and Two Buffalo or Tom didn't speak Spanish. Giving up on communicating with the Comancheros, they herded them to the prisoner cave and locked them in one of the cages. Tom tossed some items to them that could be used to bandage the wounded man.

"The two-wheel cart is missing, in the morning we will find out where it went," Tom said.

As the morning light revealed the canyon, Tom scouted the area. The caves were the only shelter. The horses were in a corral on the south side, and hay and water were brought to them. There were two caves. The larger cave held two cages for prisoners. The smaller one was filled with supplies which included food, blankets, gunpowder, lead for making bullets, and what appeared to be booty gotten from raiding travelers or homesteads.

A quarter-mile from the canyon entrance, Tom found their dump. Along with tin cans, bottles, and broken items, there lay the decaying and bloated bodies of four people. Tom guessed that three were men and the fourth a woman. Plains animals had been feeding on them. He retrieved a shovel from the supply cave and dug shallow graves for the four departed souls. After saying a few words over them, Tom walked back to the canyon. He was in a dark mood.

This disregard for human life by the Comancheros was added to the memories of the two Mexicans he found executed near the stream. He fought the urge to become judge, jury, and executioner for the men in the cage.

A study of the tracks leaving the canyon told the story of riders and two carts heading south. There were also the footprints of people being led behind the second cart.

Two Buffalo watched Tom return to the fire. "What do you want to do with the prisoners?"

"Based on what I have seen, we would be doing the world a favor by just killing them," Tom shook his head. "But we can't. That would bring us to the same level as these animals."

Two Buffalo shrugged his shoulders. "I have no problem killing them. If you like, you ride on and I will catch up."

Tom smiled, unsure if his friend was serious or not. "Nope, we will leave them in the cage, destroy their supplies, and take the horses. They will be able to break out of the cage after a day or so."

Two Buffalo chuckled, "You are a good man. I just hope it does not come back to haunt us."

The two men resupplied themselves from the Comancheros' goods. Tom chose a tall buckskin for his horse. The mule once again would carry their packs.

The Comancheros' saddles were stacked in the fire pit after having the cinch straps cut. Wood from the corral poles was piled on top of the saddles and lit. Tom emptied and damaged the extra firearms. He then dumped gunpowder over them. When lit, the sulfur and charcoal mixture flared up in a large ball of fire and smoke.

One keg of gunpowder was left in the supply cave. This would be detonated before they departed. The ignited gunpowder and the burning saddles sent plumes of smoke into the clear blue sky. Tom hoped that it would not draw others before they were done.

Filled canteens and some food were left for the six caged prisoners. Tom tested the cage bars. It would take the men some time to break out. The second cage was dragged out with horses. When they were done wrecking it, the cage was a twisted, useless pile of iron.

It was time to go. Two Buffalo started the extra horses out of the canyon. Tom went back to light the fuse on the keg. Coal oil had been poured over the remaining supplies. It would make a spectacular fire. The body of the man he had shot lay just inside the opening.

He thought about the two caves a moment before lighting the fuse. There was a possibility that the explosion would collapse both and trap the men in the cage. Tom decided to leave that to fortune. He lit the fuse, quickly mounted the buckskin and rode out of the canyon, leading Ralph.

As Tom trotted away from the opening, the powder went off. The percussion caused the buckskin and Ralph to jump into a gallop. As he rode after Two Buffalo, Tom looked back at the smoke billowing into the blue sky.

CHAPTER TWELVE

Eva sat with the other captives a short distance from the fire. The jefe had shot an elk earlier in the day and all of the Comancheros were enjoying broiled steaks. She closed her eyes and took pleasure in the aroma from the sizzling meat. Each evening a pot of boiled beans was given to them for their meal.

One day, stale bread was included. It was gotten from a small farm consisting of three adobe buildings and a rundown corral. The terrified farmer had been quick to give the Comancheros anything they wanted. The cheese and butter taken had not been shared with the captives.

The procession was a day south of Pueblo. Eva could sense fear in the others. Bottles of tequila had been picked up from a small trading post in Pueblo. It wasn't much of a town. The scattering of buildings included a trading post, a mission, a blacksmith, and some small adobe buildings occupied by the residents.

She understood the fright. Each day when Eva was taken from the cart she counted the other captives. After four days of travel, two were missing. Eva learned that if a man or woman fell, they would be left to drag behind. The two missing members had been unable to continue. One of the Comancheros had clubbed them and their bodies left along the trail.

It didn't make sense to Eva. Each of the captives was worth money when sold. She didn't understand why they would let them perish.

The Comancheros' two carts were loaded with ill-gotten trade goods. The one cart Eva rode in was filled with crated items, leaving just enough room for her. There was no room for the rest of the human cargo. They had to walk or die.

One of the women was Cheyenne, a language Eva could speak. She had told her that they were headed for Santa Fe. Once there, they would be sold and brought to Mexico. The men would be worked in mines or other heavy labor. The woman would be servants or kept by a wealthy man for entertainment. Some would be put into brothels, where their futures would be abusive and short.

Eva decided that dying while trying to escape would be better than what was in store. She would watch for the chance to get some type of weapon. One night, when the Comancheros were drinking heavily, she would go.

Less than two days ride behind Eva, Tom squinted at the heat waves on the horizon. He had a cheroot clenched in his teeth. His buckskin shirt was stained with salty sweat. The mule would occasionally tug on the lead rope, chafing Tom's leg.

He was watching for Two Buffalo's return. His friend had taken the Comancheros' horses into Pueblo. After selling them, he was to meet with Tom. The men figured that fewer questions would be asked if an Indian brought the horses in. A gringo might cause suspicion, or even a confrontation.

After crossing the Arkansas River, they were in Mexican territory. Mexico and the United State were still at odds after the Alamo four years earlier, and the subsequent defeat of Santa Anna. The Mexican government was aggressively holding on to their claim. Much of the area was ruled by the Comanche. The area was known as Comancheria. Trade between the Comanche and Comancheros included weapons, household goods, and slaves. Not all Comancheros treated captives as badly as the ones they were following. But all of them ruled their territory using intimidation.

Tom should have been enjoying the area around him. The high desert was covered with black-eyed susan, paintbrush, milkweed, rabbitbrush, and tumbleweed. Several wild grasses grew, offering grazing for the buckskin and Ralph. The mountains were to the west and a majestic butte rose to the south. Sandstone pillars stood as evidence of the eroding winds.

His thoughts weren't on the landscape, as he was worried about Two Buffalo. He should have come back by now. The carts of the Comancheros were getting closer and Tom didn't have time to look for

Two Buffalo. Yet he knew that he could not leave his friend behind.

The summer temperatures were in the nineties and the sun blazed down on Tom. The rivers had adequate water, but many of the smaller streams had stopped flowing, offering only a few pools of water. Dust devils played on the hazy horizon.

During the chase after the Comancheros, Tom and Two Buffalo had come across the bodies of two of the captives. Each time he'd feared that the body would be Eva's. After the bodies had been buried, Tom vowed that he would make them pay for what they were doing.

It was mid-afternoon when Tom spotted a rider in the distance obscured by rising heatwaves. The rider was moving slowly and slumped over the pommel of the saddle.

Tom spurred the buckskin into a cantor. The mule pulled back and then consented to the faster pace. Tom recognized Two Buffalo's paint. He released Ralph and galloped to meet his friend. He rode alongside the paint and took the reins.

Two Buffalo was semi-conscious. He had tied his hands to the saddle to prevent falling off. His face was badly bruised, and there was a large bump on his forehead. Tom swung down. Cutting Two Buffalo's hands free, he lowered him onto the ground. A quick check confirmed that there were no bullet wounds.

He raised Two Buffalo's head and tried to get him to drink some water, then carried him to the shade of a dwarfed cottonwood tree. Ignoring the horses for a moment, he poured water onto his neckerchief and bathed the cuts and bruises on Two Buffalo's face.

Once Tom was convinced that Two Buffalo had no serious cuts or broken bones, he left him lying under the tree and went to get the animals. They were browsing on whatever they could find, and dragging their reins. Once he had the gear off the horses and mule, he started a small fire to make a jerky broth.

He looked over and saw that Two Buffalo was looking at him.

"How are you feeling?" Tom asked.

"Angry!" was the answer Tom got in return.

Tom added a few things to the pot and turned to his friend. "What happened?"

Two Buffalo moved a bit to get more comfortable. "I was not careful. I sold the horses and decided to pick up a few things we could use. Some men were hanging around in front of the trading post. They saw my strong medicine necklace and my money."

"I left the trading post and led my horse to a grove of trees to have a quick meal. I saw the men ride west toward some sandstone cliffs. I finished eating and headed out to meet you."

"They were waiting for me. One of the men rode out, blocking my way, while the other rode up behind me. Before I could react, they jumped me. I was hit several times and kicked. Being on my back on the ground, I could not fight back. They grabbed the necklace and my saddle bags with the money."

"We can manage without the money from the horses, and we can replace the items in your saddle bags," Tom assured his friend. "Having you back here is the most important thing."

"I have the money and the necklace," Two Buffalo said. "When they left, I followed them. When I caught up to the men, they came at me, one firing his rifle and missing. They should have taken my horse and gun, I shot into one before the second was on me. He hit me with the barrel of his rifle. Again, I was on the ground. He jumped down to finish me and I put my knife in him."

"Once I got our money and the necklace, I was able to get back on the horse. My head was spinning from the knock with the gun barrel. I tied my hands in case I blacked out. I was hopeful that the paint would find you."

Tom looked at the tough, old Cheyenne. Last winter, he had met this man waiting to die in his death lodge. Eight months later, his will to live was strong.

By the next morning, Two Buffalo was ready to go on. His cheek was cut and bruised and he had a nice goose egg on his forehead, but his determination to help a friend save a woman drove him on.

* * *

As the two men moved out to continue their quest, Eva sat in the jarring cart and slowly searched through the load. Once, when a wheel bounced over a rock, one of the crates slid, trapping her against the sideboards. It was wedged, and when she tried to move the crate would not budge.

Briefly, panic swept through her. The crate pressed heavily on her and breathing was difficult. A vision of her lifeless body lying on the trail flashed through her mind. Again, the cart lurched. The crate moved enough to free her.

Pushing it into a more secure place, Eva continued to look for any sharp or pointed object. Finally, her search was rewarded. One of the crates had a mirror. It had broken with all the movement and a four-inch long shard protruded from between two boards.

Carefully, she removed the sharp glass. This would allow her to cut the bonds. The longer she waited, the further south she would be. Eva decided that she would attempt to escape as early as tonight.

With the sun low in the western sky, the cart stopped, and there was the usual shouting as the captives were moved to a secure area. The back of her cart was opened and a greasy and dust-covered man reached in and pulled her out.

Eva had hidden the glass in the folds of her gingham dress. She looked around the camp as the man pushed her toward the others. While riding in the covered cart, Eva had watched through the cracks in the side board and had committed much of the area traveled to memory.

About five miles back there was a dried riverbed that cut into the cliffs to the west. While it would not be difficult to travel on foot, it appeared that a rider would have trouble.

The evening soup was brought and the captives pressed together, trying to make sure their clay bowls were filled before it was gone. A bucket of water sat near the soup. Once the soup had been eaten a short, fat man with drooping wool britches came to collect the bowls.

Tom and Two Buffalo had made good time, closing the distance between them and the carts. While riding across the desert plain, they had to keep a sharp lookout for Comanche or Comancheros. Both were equally dangerous. The Mexican Army rode in dusty groups and could be seen at a distance, thus avoided.

At dusk the two men rode up a rise, which offered some protection against the wind coming in from the west. It was an overcast night and the moon offered no light. Supper was made over a small fire, using wood that had been collected during the day and carried on Ralph.

The rise sloped down to the northwest, creating a shelf that had a fair amount of grass. A spring provided water for the grass and had a small pool for watering the animals. The mule and horses were rubbed down and picketed for the night.

With the animals taken care of, Tom got back just as Two Buffalo finished making supper. In a Dutch oven taken from the Comancheros' supplies, he had made cornbread. One of the things Two Buffalo had brought back from Pueblo was some mild, soft cheese. This was spread over the steaming cornbread and washed down with hot, strong coffee.

Tom lay awake late that night. If the Comancheros weren't overtaken before Santa Fe it was unlikely he would be able to rescue Eva. Once Santa Fe was reached the human cargo would be sold off first and then sent to all corners of Mexico.

Being a gringo, Tom couldn't travel freely looking for information. He figured the distance was still over a week's travel from Santa Fe. It should be plenty of time to catch up.

Less than seven miles away, unknown to Tom, Eva was planning her escape. Eva had noticed that the men would leave the canteen sitting in the cart. It would be filled each morning for her. She had conserved water and knew it was over half-full.

A cold breeze was blowing, so the captives huddled together to share warmth. The sky was cloud-covered. The nearly full moon would be hidden tonight. Eva sat near the edge of the captives and watched the Comancheros drink themselves into a stupor.

It was late when the men started to go to their blankets. The jefe went to sleep earlier after checking over the cargo and the captives. Four of the Comancheros continued to drink. Some of these would be the men who would relieve the two guards watching them.

One of their guards shouted something at the four men. Eva guessed that they wanted to be relieved. The other captives lay together sleeping. Eva watched as two of the drunken guards came to watch them.

One sat on the back of the open cart and cleaned his gun. The other sat leaning against a boulder, out of the wind. Eva heard him start snoring. The guard on the cart looked over. Grunting, he stood to go and wake his companion. Eva sat up suddenly and stretched, thrusting her bosom against the thin gingham dress, hoping to get his attention.

The guard stopped and looked at her. She nodded at him and smiled. She had cut the bond off her wrists and ankles. Holding her untied wrists together, she slowly rubbed her hands down her legs. The guard looked at her and then at the other sleeping man.

Eva motioned him over. Glancing at the men sleeping at the fire, he decided it was safe. The guard placed his rifle against the cart and strutted over to Eva. She tilted her head, looking up at him and smiling.

He leaned down with a grin that showed his broken teeth. He grabbed her arm to help her up. As she came up, Eva thrust the sharp glass point into his throat. Shock and confusion crossed his face as he grabbed for the glass. Eva pulled him down on top of her and held him while he quickly bled out.

Eva was thankful that the man died without crying out. She was lucky that the sharp glass had cut the artery and lodged in the vocal cords. Pushing the man off her, Eva took his knife. Turning, she saw the wide eyes of the other captives. Quickly, she decided that they could not be left.

Cautioning them to be quiet, she took the guards knife and cut the bonds of one of the young men. She motioned him to free the rest. Moving on cat feet, she got the canteen and rifle from the cart. When she got back to the others, Eva saw that the young man had also taken the powder horns and gun belt from the dead man.

Checking the snoring guard, Eva debated whether it was worth taking a chance killing him for his weapons. She decided that it was not. Quietly, the freed captives moved north into the high desert.

The bucket had some water left and was taken along with the canteen. Water had not been a problem on the main trail, but she dared not follow that. What little water they had, and luck, would have to prevent the group from perishing from thirst on the high desert.

The cold wind made their teeth chatter as the small assembly walked quickly. It was imperative that distance was put between them and their captors before their escape was discovered. Eva wished she had the stars to guide her. But with the stars would come moonlight, making finding them easier.

She kept the wind to her left side. That would keep them in the general northerly direction. Eva led the group. She realized that since her father had traded her, Eva had let others direct her. It had just caused her trouble. If there was to be trouble, Eva thought, she would bring it on herself.

Light was not yet showing in the east when the cold and tired group reached the dry riverbed. Eva knew that on foot they could not outrun the Comancheros. Hiding was their only chance. Traveling through the boulder-strewn riverbed was slow. Eva warned the others about being careless and leaving too much sign to follow.

With stubbed toes, barked shins, and scraped hands, the fleeing men and women continued climbing through the riverbed. The steep walls rising on both sides offered them some protection. Eva was aware that they had left without food to sustain them while traveling.

Unaware of how close they were to those who could help, they progressed through the cluttered ravine. Tom was almost sleeping when he came wide awake. Someone, or something, was moving out there.

He lay still, listening for the sound again. It may have been an animal looking their camp over. He wished that he had the dog.

The desperate escapees consisted of five women, including Eva, and six men. The men were all Mexican or Spanish. The women were a mix of Mexican and Cheyenne. They struggled in the dark, moving along the difficult riverbed. The warmth of the morning sun was welcome to them. Soon, the sun burned through the haze and make the river gorge feel like an oven. In the high desert, the nights brought the cold and days the heat. Each person took a small drink of water.

While they rested for a few minutes, Eva heard the sound of galloping horses. It came from the top of the river gorge on the south side. There was an undercut from past floods on the south cliff and they moved quickly to hide under its edge. Eva listened as the riders went by. She knew the Comancheros might send some to ride west and watch the gorge for anyone trying to make their way down.

A short distance away, Two Buffalo was up early and heated water for tea. "There is nothing like cold cornbread with hot tea," he declared.

"I could use some strong coffee," Tom complained. "I didn't sleep well. There were noises that kept me awake."

"The tea will be strong," Two Buffalo assured him. "I am glad you are sleeping light again, I also heard something. It moved in the riverbed below."

The cliff above the riverbed was 30 paces from their camp. Tom strolled over to the cliff edge and looked down. The water had left behind a field of boulders, from the size of a pumpkin to the size of a milk cow. He watched until Two Buffalo called him to breakfast.

He accepted the cup of tea. Blowing softly to cool it off, Tom took a sip. It was sweet!

Two Buffalo smiled as he watched Tom's face. "You like the tea?"

"Damn good tea," Tom replied. "You got some honey in town, didn't you?"

The men were saddling the horses when they heard the riders. The sound was coming from the other side of the river gorge. Tom moved up to the ridge and looked across. Two men that looked like Comancheros were riding along the south edge, searching for something in the riverbed.

Tom scanned the area around them for any other movement. He spotted dust in two other areas. It could be dust devils or riders. He was not sure. They had ridden about two miles down the dry river to reach the spot that protected them from the wind. Watching the dust for a moment more, he realized it was riders and that they were near the dry river crossing, coming down this side.

Tom hurried down to the horses. Two Buffalo was just finishing packing the mule.

"We got to move," Tom said. "We got riders coming this way."

Tom and Two Buffalo rode hard, away from the horsemen. They kept to the lower areas to try and keep from being seen.

Eva moved the tired and hungry group out from the undercut. She now feared that it was a mistake. She had led them into a gorge that had no exit, except continuing down. If discovered, those above could systematically pick them off with rifles.

The sound of more horses came from above the gorge. This time the riders were on the north side. The trap was being set for them. Only two of the woman spoke Cheyenne, and the rest of the group spoke Spanish. Eva wished that they all could discuss a plan. As long as there was freedom, there should be a way out.

Darkness would be the only chance. The water was gone, and the riverbed offered nothing to eat or drink so far. The group continued down the gorge, watching for anyone from above. Finally, a pool of water was found.

Eva hissed a warning. "Come here. We need to make sure it is safe," she said, pressing against the side of the rocky wall.

Most of the men and women hurried to the pool, crouching and scooping the water. Two rifle shots echoed loudly in the gorge.

Screaming, the terrified group scattered, looking for shelter from an unseen enemy. Two men lay at the pool's edge, their life blood spreading on the water. Eva crouched on the south wall and was sure that the shots came from above her. She shouted at the others to come her way.

It was no use, they were in a panic. Another shot rang out, knocking a young girl among the boulders. The shot was followed by several more that were near-misses, showering the scrambling victims with pieces of rock and fragments of bullets. The shrieks of terror were deafening.

Tom heard the gunshots. He looked at Two Buffalo, who was pointing toward the gorge. Sliding off the horses, the two men ran to the rim of the gorge. The screams of those below rose to greet them. Two Comancheros were intent on their shooting on the opposite rim. The men were toying with those remaining below.

Tom and Two Buffalo readied their rifles. "On my command we fire," Tom said.

"Now!" The long rifle and Hawken spoke with authority, and the two men across the gorge dropped in their tracks. The cries below continued.

Tom could see the three horsemen riding hard after them. One was waving a hand gun over his head. Tom moved to the edge and called out to find out if Eva was below.

"Eva! Eva, can you hear me!"

Before an answer came up, the three riders began to fire.

Eva strained her ears. She had heard someone call her name. She stepped out to look. Those still alive were crouching and whimpering behind whatever cover was available. There were more shots, and she threw herself back against the wall. The shots were on the north wall.

Two Buffalo had the long rifle reloaded and took aim. His shot knocked one of the riders to the ground, bouncing and rolling.

Tom finished loading the Hawken and took aim. The two remaining riders had dismounted and were ducking for cover. Tom squeezed the shot off just as the lagging man jumped. By the way he jerked, Tom was sure he had put lead into him.

Two Buffalo set his long rifle down and, pulling his knife, disappeared into the rocks. Tom moved back near the gorge.

Again, he called, "Eva, are you down there?"

Eva looked up at the man standing at the rim. She couldn't believe her eyes. It was the tall man. "Yes, yes I am!" she shouted back.

"Stay where you are, we will keep you covered from here," Tom called back.

He disappeared from the rim. Eva moved out and got the remaining men and women together. Anger surged through her as she looked at four innocent people lying dead. Three of the remaining survivors had severe lacerations from the ricocheting bullets.

Tom moved slowly in the direction where the men had disappeared. He could see the first man Two Buffalo had shot. He was crawling on his belly, heading for some rocks for cover. He had a six gun in his hand.

The wounded man was 40 paces from Tom. Carefully, he lined up on the man with his Colt. Squeezing off a shot, he showered the man with dirt as the bullet hit in front of him. Tom was aiming dead center, but the handgun didn't have the accuracy of the Hawken.

The man lay flat, covering his face. "You move and the next one will be through you!" Tom threatened. If the man continued to move, Tom would put one from the rifle into him.

A cry came from the direction where the other riders had gone. Tom watched intently toward the sound. Finally, he saw Two Buffalo stand up, holding a scalp. He was waving at Tom to join him.

Tom trotted closer while keeping an eye on his wounded man lying on the ground. He stepped around the up-thrust rocks and saw Two Buffalo standing over a dead Comanchero.

"I didn't know you were a scalp-hunting Cheyenne," Tom chided Two Buffalo.

Tossing the scalp aside, Two Buffalo smiled. "I noticed this man had scalps on his belt. I thought I would add his to it. The other one you fired at is lying behind the rocks, with a ball through his hips."

It took Tom and Two Buffalo a few minutes to get the wounded prisoners tied up and the horses together. Fortunately, all of the Comancheros' horses carried leather riatas.

Tom gathered up the riatas and went to the gorge. Eva had the remaining men and women together and had done her best to stop the bleeding. Their searing thirst forced them to drink the bloodied water.

The gorge wall had cracks that would allow footholds. Tom tied the leather ropes together, and slowly the seven remaining people were brought up from the riverbed. Eva came up last, and when she appeared over the edge the tall man spoke to her.

"My name is Tom Franklin. I and my friend, Two Buffalo, have come to get you."

Eva smiled and sank to the ground. The strength she had gained from being responsible for the group had gone, and a weakness washed over her. She sat because she didn't trust her legs to hold her.

Tom knelt next to her. "Are you hurt?"

"No, I am okay, just very tired," she replied.

CHAPTER THIRTEEN

Eva watched as Tom prepared to take them with him. There was a total of nine people, including Tom and Two Buffalo. They had five horses and one mule. Eva glanced at the two horses standing on the other side of the gorge. She realized that it would take over an hour to go and get them. It was too much time. The horses on their side would have to do.

Tom stripped the pack gear off the mule and switched his saddle to it. He then put a Comanchero's saddle on the buckskin. Two Buffalo looked sadly at the Dutch oven they had just gotten at the caves that would be left behind. The pack rig replaced the saddle on the Comanchero's horse. It would help the riders hang on.

Each of the rescued people was given jerky to chew, and water. Two Buffalo took out the last of the cornbread and cheese to share.

The group rode out with Two Buffalo on the paint and Tom on the mule. Eva rode the buckskin and a man and woman rode double on each of the Comanchero's horses. Tom led the group directly north. Disarmed and untied, the wounded Comanchero shouted at them as they rode away.

The vision of the bodies lying in the riverbed left Tom feeling uncomfortable. They were victims of cruel men who dealt in enslaving people for profit. Time wouldn't allow burying them. He made them a silent promise that if the other Comancheros caught up with them, he would do everything he could to give those killed justice. It would be an eye for an eye.

Eva looked at the broad shoulders of the man who led them. Her heart beat a bit faster when she thought about a possible future with him. It made sense. He'd come all the way down here to bring her back. He must want her. She worried about Samuel. When they got back, he might claim his rights.

The group stayed ahead of any pursuit the first day. The people with Eva needed a good meal before they moved on. That evening, Two Buffalo broiled steaks from a deer he'd shot earlier with his bow. A thick pot of bean soup seasoned with wild onions and molasses bubbled on the fire. Hot coffee sweetened with honey finished off the meal.

Eva sat by Tom, drinking her coffee. He had more lines around his eyes than she remembered. It was probably the strain of hunting for her. When he removed his hat, she could see the fresh scar showing through his brown hair from a bullet wound

"When we get back, Samuel will be waiting for me," she told him.

Shaking his head, he looked into her eyes. "He won't be waiting. The Mexicans killed him and took what was left of the money."

Eva sat back, thinking about what he had just told her. It meant that she was free to decide her own future. She glanced back at Tom. She hoped that she was looking at her future.

Tom woke to get everyone up two hours before sunrise. He noticed that Two Buffalo was already awake and had a small fire for coffee. After a quick breakfast, everyone was in the saddle and riding north.

By evening the group was crossing the Arkansas River. This would mean that United States territory was reached. This brought little comfort to Tom. The Comancheros behind them raided north of the river. Even now, it would be two days' ride north before reaching the area where the caves were located.

Tom and Two Buffalo had taken food enough for the two of them, figuring on a little supplemental hunting. Now, there were nine eating. Tom worried about running out before reaching safety. Water holes, rivers, and streams were plentiful enough, so water would not be an issue. Tom was thankful that available water wouldn't dictate the route. With water widely available, their route could not be anticipated by the Comancheros.

The next night, camp was on a stream with a line of live oak trees. The stream was a trickle, but the camp was next to a deep, cold pool. Tom watched as Eva got the fire going. She sent the Mexican men to catch fish. Tom provided them line and hooks.

Tom rode to a rise to watch the back trail. Lying on the ridge watching south, he wondered if there would be a time when a person could live a relaxed lifestyle and not worry about what might come over the next rise.

The setting sun put on a fiery display in the west. Slowly, the shadows grew long on the high desert floor. Tom waited until a half-hour after full dark and saw no fires. Maybe the Comancheros wouldn't consider them worth chasing.

Eva proudly showed Tom the tin plateful of broiled trout that she'd saved for him. "The men had good success fishing. There is still enough for the morning."

Tom took the plate and sat just a little way from the fire. Eva poured a cup of coffee and brought it to him. She sat close, and he could smell the freshness of her body. She and the others had taken the opportunity to bathe. Tom's mind was filled with thoughts of their future while he ate the sweet-tasting fish.

"Have we lost the Comancheros?" Eva asked.

"We make too many tracks to lose them. We can hope they decided not to follow," he said.

Eva took the empty plate and brought it to one of the girls to clean. She moved to refill Tom's cup. The firelight reflected off her skin. The gingham dress clung to the gentle curves of her body. Eva returned with the coffee and again sat near him. As Tom took the cup, his hand brushed Eva's. He fought the urge to put his arm around her. It would be forward of him to do so.

Eva sat quietly, wanting to say something. Inside, she felt like she was about to burst. This man beside her had a difficult job in front of him and couldn't be distracted by a chatty female. She vowed that when they were away from danger, there would be much she would say to him.

Looking at Tom, Eva noticed a bit of fish hanging on his beard. "Let me help you a second," she said, and brushed the meat away. "Just a bit of fish."

Tom looked over and smiled. "Thank you, Eva."

She felt the warmth of his body as he moved a bit closer.

Tom woke before sunrise and took advantage of the pond. Back in Vermont, the family had bathed once a week, on Saturday. In the summer, during haying, a bath was taken mid-week also. On many hot nights he and Isaac would swim in the Connecticut River.

Daylight found them moving north again. The comfort and beauty of the shaded pond was quickly replaced with the blazing sun and grey-green desert plants. Heat waves made the horizon dance. Tom swung a little east, to put distance between the Comancheros' caves and themselves.

Eva continued to keep the men and women moving. Tom was pleased that she took charge of watching over them. He was focused on their direction and watching for danger. Two Buffalo searched for game. Each day, he managed to bring something back. To avoid noise, he was using the bow.

The group had found water in the late afternoon. It was too early to stop. Tom had them water the stock and fill the canteens. There was a leather water bag on one of the Comancheros' horses. Its contents would be used for cooking.

A dry camp was made that night. The fire was kept small. The camp was in the open, with higher land on the west and north. The fire was shielded from the south using a large boulder. Everyone was hot and tired. Before the heat of the day had left the ground, most were sleeping.

Tom wanted to take advantage of the cool morning. Again, the party moved out at first light. Eva rode next to Tom. He was leading them to Fort William, or any U.S. Army detail they met along the way. It was still five days to the fort. Tom finally had hope that they might make it, if the horses could hold up.

It was full light when Two Buffalo pointed to the dust of horses following them. Tom spurred his horse to a rise for a better look. Maybe it was some U.S. troops on patrol. Squinting in the early morning light, he could see the ragged line of riders. It was not the U.S. Army.

By noon, the pursuit was only two hours behind them. Tom had to make a decision. Their horses were in no shape to outrun the Comancheros. He would have to go back and counter-attack. It would give the others time to put distance between themselves and the pursuers.

Tom outlined the plan. Eva's face was grave. Two Buffalo insisted on joining him. Placing the necklace on his chest, he looked sternly at his friend.

"You and I have come a long way to live or die together. You found me in the wilderness and fed me for the winter so I could live. I killed the big cat that attacked you so you could live. If we are to die today, we will travel together on the other side."

Tom saw tears in Eva's eyes as she listened to Two Buffalo's speech. While transferring items from the mule and the paint, she walked up beside him.

"I need you to lead these people to Fort William," Tom told her.

"I do not want to leave you . . . too lose you again," she pleaded.

Smiling, Tom put his arm around her, holding her close. "I have much to live for with you, Eva. I will return and meet you at the fort." He then kissed her softly on the lips.

Swinging into the saddle, he and Two Buffalo rode south without looking back. Eva knew that she was once again responsible for the lives of these people. Turning the buckskin north, she led the way at a trot, her heart heavy.

Tom and Two Buffalo both carried two rifles and three handguns. With the two rifles, it would give them the chance to fire several shots while the Comancheros were still a distance away. Once the fight was in close quarters, the handguns would be emptied. And then, Tom knew, death would follow. It was worth dying to give Eva and the others a chance to escape.

Two Buffalo spoke while staring straight ahead at the riders. "If we strike and run, we can make the Comancheros follow us. It will take them off the others' trail."

Tom looked around for a defendable position. In the distance, and northeast, he could see a small plateau. He estimated that it was about five miles away. He looked at Two Buffalo's paint, and Ralph. The animals had lost weight during the trip. If they could prevent a full gallop, the animals should be able to make the run.

Tom pointed to a cluster of boulders a mile east. Two Buffalo nodded and turned the paint. They rode toward the boulders. The Comancheros adjusted their angle and continued after the two men. It would be at least an hour before the advancing party would be in range.

Reaching the boulders, Tom was pleased to see that it was defendable, with protection for their animals. In the shade of the tallest boulder there was some grass growing.

While the horse and mule grazed, Tom and Two Buffalo climbed onto the larger boulders. The field of fire would be good. Continuing on lathered horses, the Comancheros came on.

Tom could plainly see the man who the men called jefe. Eva had told them that the man's name was Este Santos. He commanded the area north of the Arkansas River and south of the Platte. Most of the area was inhabited by plains tribes. Este would make excursions east, west and south of the caves, stealing, killing and trading.

The oncoming Comancheros were a quarter-mile away. Tom decided to try hitting one of them with the Hawken rifle. When he was with Gus and Hector, they would break up the monotony by shooting at long-range targets. Gus had always won. Today, Tom needed to win.

They estimated that there were 12 to 15 horsemen. Several riders were behind the jefe. That would be his target. He would hopefully hit one behind him if he missed Este Santos. Taking a deep breath and slowly exhaling, Tom feathered the forward trigger. The Hawken jumped against his shoulder. A couple seconds later a horse to the left of jefe went down, sending its rider rolling. With the horse down, several others swerved their horses to avoid the downed animal and man.

The Comancheros dismounted and spread out, seeking cover. Some returned fire, their shots hitting short. Tom knew that it would only be moments before they found the range.

"Now we lessen their willingness to follow us," Two Buffalo said, lining up on a bush a Comanchero ducked behind. He squeezed the long rifle trigger, hoping to at least put the ball close to the man.

Tom lifted his second rifle and fired at a man running low to the right. The running man dropped to the ground, disappearing from sight.

Tom had set down gunpowder wrapped in newspaper for reloading. Tearing the end off, he poured the measured amount of powder down the barrel. Placing a greased patch over the bore, he rammed the ball down the Hawken barrel. He set the cap and aimed. The action took less than 15 seconds.

Tom fired again. For a moment nothing happened, and then a man appeared, running for alternate cover. He took a few steps before collapsing headlong onto the ground. As fast at the two could load, they fired at the Comancheros. There was no longer anyone who wanted to take a chance of showing themselves.

The rifle fire coming from the Comancheros whined away as the balls hit the boulders Tom and Two Buffalo hid behind. Some of the shots were coming from much closer. The Comancheros were working their way toward the boulders.

"Let's go," Tom whispered.

Scrambling off the boulders, Tom and Two Buffalo mounted their animals and rode away, keeping the boulders to cover their exit. There was a shout from the Comancheros. Their move had been seen. Tom looked back and the wind took off his hat, sending it cartwheeling along the ground.

Cussing at the loss, Tom rode low in the saddle and headed for the small plateau with Two Buffalo. It rose from a mound of earth and had the appearance of a fortress or castle. The extra rifles had been left behind to save weight. The paint and Ralph needed every advantage that they could get.

A good eighth of a mile was gained by using the boulders for cover. The Comancheros lost additional time gathering up their scattered mounts. A second factor in their favor was the present condition of the Comancheros' horses. Having been run hard, their pace had slowed and the two men were able to gain distance.

It took 30 minutes to reach the plateau. The paint and mule were all but exhausted. Tom looked back and saw that many of their pursuers had dropped out of the chase and had stopped, or were walking their horses. As he watched, one of the men's horses collapsed from being pushed, sending the Comanchero sprawling to the desert floor.

Tom and Two Buffalo led their mounts up the mound, allowing them to walk and get some kind of breather. Both animals had been lathered and breathing heavily when they reached the base of the plateau.

The mound had a few evergreens and some good depressions to give them cover. At the rock wall there was an undercut. A small pool of water had collected and was still there because it was shaded by trees and the wind could not reach it. Tom and Two Buffalo drank first and topped off their canteens. The thirsty animals drank the remaining water.

They put the horse and mule under the ledge near the rock wall. The animals stood with their heads hanging, exhausted from the run. The shadows and brush would hide them from the enemy below.

The top of the plateau leaned to one side. It might be possible to climb.

"I think we should try and get to the top and fire from there," Tom suggested.

"I am Cheyenne. We stay low so we can move. At the top, Comancheros could leave a couple men to keep us trapped, and the rest could ride after Eva and the others," Two Buffalo wisely said.

Tom nodded in agreement. "Good thinking, which is why you are the teacher."

Two Buffalo held his rifle with a proud look on his face. Tom wished that he could catch that look on a tin type and keep it forever.

Shrugging, Tom thought, Forever for us could be just a few hours.

The Comancheros assembled out of rifle range, planning strategy for the attack. Tom noticed that the jefe stayed well to the back. He would settle for sending his subordinates to face their rifles.

Two Buffalo watched the Comancheros below. He could see the tension on Tom's face. Maybe talking would help while waiting for the attack.

"We are in my people's land," Two Buffalo said.

"I thought they were further north," Tom replied.

"That too," the old Cheyenne said. "We range from the Arkansas River and north beyond the Platte. We share the area with the Arapahoe. The Lakota are on our northern edge and the Crow and Flathead are to the west. Most often we fight each other, except when it is time to hunt buffalo."

"Now we are fighting each other less because we have a common enemy. It is the white man who wants our land and game. The white man comes and digs in the rocks for gold and silver. He ignores what the good earth provides, and will replenish."

"Man cannot eat the gold or silver. He can only buy things that he does not need."

Tom realized that Two Buffalo was not criticizing him. Rather, he had accepted their fate against the Comancheros and wanted to share inner thoughts with him.

"Sometimes the gold and silver can be for good," Tom said. "Some men use it to help others, to build towns and provide jobs for other families."

"Hmm," Two Buffalo replied, "the good earth will provide this for man, without building towns. Man should move over the earth and leave no mark behind, except his good deeds that will be talked about around the winter fires."

Tom knew that they were coming from two different cultures, that cold and hunger during the winter and plenty in the summer was accepted by Two Buffalo's people. It was hard to explain the benefit of warm houses in the winter and food for purchase year-round.

The Comancheros had stopped short of the plateau and were starting to spread out. They would surround the earth mound and work their way closer to Tom and Two Buffalo, using the same cover that the two men used to defend the position.

Tom was ready with his Hawken rifle. He saw a tight group of three men moving about an eighth of a mile away. Adjusting for distance and their elevation, Tom gently squeezed off a shot.

Two men hit the ground while the other jumped for cover. One got up holding his arm and ran for some rocks. The other remained on the ground. A hail of searching fire was directed at the mound from the other Comancheros.

"A .50 caliber bullet makes a nice, large hole," Two Buffalo said with satisfaction. He flinched as one of the Comancheros bullets hit a bit too close for comfort, and then aimed the long rifle at a bunch of horses. Firing, he wounded one, scattering the rest kicking and running.

With the Hawken rifle reloaded, Tom fired at another bunch of horses. He scored a hit, sending them running. The Comancheros pulled back to catch the fleeing horses and moved the rest back.

"We bought some time." Tom said.

The sun was low in the sky. Soon it would be dark, and the men below would work their way up the mound. The Comancheros might work closely with the Comanche, but they did not have the stealth. Their method was to bully and intimidate people, depending on superior numbers and ruthlessness to win.

Tom and Two Buffalo watched their clumsy attempts to gain access to the mound. A few well-placed shots would drive them back out of range. They did not take the Comancheros lightly. While there had been success this afternoon, the men below would soon come up with a strategy that would defeat their position.

It could be as simple as water and food. The side of the plateau was to the west. The afternoon sun had been brutal. Using their water sparingly, Tom knew that it would be gone by the next day.

"After dark, we will separate," Two Buffalo said. "The Comancheros know our current position and will work their way to it in the dark. We can use the knife and reduce their numbers. By daylight, we can be back together on the mound, ready to defend our position."

Tom nodded in agreement, chewed some jerky and sipped a little water. The sun would be down soon. He and Two Buffalo would become the hunters.

Tom watched his friend disappear to the right of the mound. He could see the Comancheros had moved off a safe distance and were sitting around a fire and enjoying some type of steaks, maybe one of the horses that had been shot. He was sure that guards remained in hiding.

CHAPTER FOURTEEN

Eva had heard the shooting after they had left. She had a strong desire to turn around and join Tom in the fight. It would have done little good and would have gone against Tom's wishes. She had thought for a moment. Was she back to being controlled, told what to do, without free will?

"No, you're not!" Eva scolded herself. "Tom, and the people with me, are depending on me. I will lead them to safety."

The young Mexican man and woman riding next to her looked over, confused over what she was saying. Smiling, Eva shook her head and motioned them to go on.

The sun was low in the western sky when Eva saw the smoke of a fire to her east. It could be Comancheros, or others just as bad. Maybe it was buffalo hunters. She stared, trying to decide what to do.

Darkness engulfed the plain and on the mound the stars offered the only light. Tom worked his way partway down, to the left of their former position. He found a spot offering cover. The moon wouldn't be rising for several more hours. When up, it would be near full. To hide, they would have to stick to the shadows.

The night passed slowly. The sound of additional horses and the creak of a two-wheel cart were heard. The added danger didn't help Tom as he fought the urge to sleep. Several times he had heard what sounded like muffled cries. Suddenly, he was wide awake. There was movement in front of him. Pushing deeper into the shadows, Tom watched and waited. It was two men working their way up the mound.

Tom touched the Colt in his holster. If he used it, he would most certainly get both men. He would also give his position away to any others within rifle range. He watched as the two men worked their way past him. They were crouching, and moving a few steps at a time.

There was a large rock between the men and their destination. Tom followed them on cat feet. His knife was drawn, and the Colt was free to be pulled if necessary. Luck was with him. The two men split, each going around opposite sides of the large rock.

He closed in quickly on the man on the right, using the method taught by Two Buffalo. He clamped his hand over the man's mouth and thrust the knife upward under his ribcage. Holding his quarry tightly, Tom felt the man struggle briefly before collapsing.

There was a soft hiss from the other man. Tom moved around the rock, crouching in a similar manner. Satisfied, the other man continued moving ahead. Again, he grabbed from the back, but this man twisted like a cat, deflecting the direction of knife thrust. It sunk into the man's side, not a killing spot. Desperately, Tom fought to keep his hand over the man's mouth, wrestling him to the ground knocking his firearm loose. They rolled down the mound. He fought to keep the man from shouting. He struggled to get his knife out of the man's side and complete the killing thrust.

Suddenly, the knife came free from the man's side as they rolled again. He now had both hands on the man, one over the man's mouth and the other holding his knife against the chest. Moving it up quickly, Tom attempted to cut the man's throat. He could hear gurgling as the sharp blade cut through the man's windpipe. The Comanchero was fighting for his life, spraying blood and froth everywhere as he gasped through the open gash in his throat. Tom could feel him weaken and brought the knife down, thrusting it under the ribcage. Soon, the man lay still.

Tom was covered with blood and physically exhausted. He rolled away from the body and curled up in some shadows. His breaths were coming in ragged pants, and his heart was pounding in his ears. Tom knew that he would easily be discovered by anyone within 30 feet. He pulled the Colt. He hadn't the strength for another fight without a little rest.

Tom heard shooting near the Comancheros' camp and saw flames from the guns stabbing out into the dark. Praying that his friend had not been caught in the open, he slowly moved back up the mound, searching for deeper shadows. He used handfuls of pine needles to rub the man's blood off his hands, arms, and clothing.

The night dragged on, with the stars and moon slowly marching across the sky. Once again, sleep was the enemy. Tom moved slowly towards the point of their defense. He needed a drink of water. The night air was cold on his shoulders. He would get the poncho off the mule.

As Tom slipped the poncho on, he heard the call of a dove not 50 feet away. Was it Two Buffalo? They had neglected to come up with a signaling method when coming back. Tom tried to make the sound of a dove in return. He heard the movement of someone coming toward him.

"You will have to work on the dove call," Two Buffalo whispered.

Tom joined him, glad to have another set of ears and eyes to help. The darkness could be a friend, but as a man's mind became too active it became a terrible thing.

"Help yourself to coffee and beans," Two Buffalo said quietly as he handed something to Tom.

It was a warm pot of coffee. Two Buffalo set a pot of beans between them and gave Tom a spoon. Drinking the coffee from the pot and hungrily eating beans, Tom questioned Two Buffalo, "How did you get these?"

"They were just sitting there," Two Buffalo said calmly. "It looked like they were done eating, so I brought them to us."

"And the gunshots?"

"Maybe a couple men had not eaten."

For the rest of the night, the two men took turns sleeping in short spells. Tom woke to the gentle shake of Two Buffalo's hand and saw that the eastern sky was just getting light.

"It is time for us to move the animals and ourselves to the east side of the plateau," Two Buffalo suggested.

Shaking the sleep from his eyes, Tom agreed.

The paint and Ralph walked quietly as Tom and Two Buffalo led them around the mound. The morning shadows made their move invisible.

"It will be warmer when the full sun is up," Tom mentioned.

"That is true," Two Buffalo said, "and the little cannon won't know where to find us."

Tom's jaw dropped and he looked, seeing the small cannon sitting in the middle of the Comanchero's camp. Just beyond the camp was a two-wheel cart. It must have been following the others, carrying the cannon. He estimated that an additional 20 men had come in last night.

Soon after the sun was full up, the Comancheros loaded the small cannon and fired at the rock wall above the two men's last known position. Rock and shell fragments showered the depression. The cannon was loaded again and fired just a bit lower, hitting the trees that the animals had just been moved from.

Tom positioned himself to fire the Hawken rifle. "The next time the cannon fires, I will try and shoot the gunner."

The cannon was loaded and aimed a little to the left. As the man put the brand to the touchhole, Tom set the action on the Hawken. As the smoke billowed out of the cannon, Tom tapped the front trigger. The gunner staggered, grabbed his chest, and fell back dead. The morning breeze quickly dispersed the plume of smoke from the Hawken.

The closest Comancheros jumped back in surprise. The men began to point in all directions, claiming to know where the shot came from. The jefe shouted out orders and the cannon was moved back another 30 yards.

Two Buffalo chuckled softly, "You got them worried, Tom Franklin."

Tom slowly surveyed the Comancheros' camp. He could see a half-dozen bodies dragged to the west side of the camp. No doubt it was some of Two Buffalo's work last night. He counted 26 men spread out below. There might be a couple more hiding on the mound. All of the horses were kept well beyond the camp, out of the range of Tom's Hawken.

It appeared that the Comancheros had food, water, and time on their side. Tom smiled, knowing that his plan appeared to have worked. Eva and the others would be another day ahead of the Comancheros. Now, he wondered, how would he and Two Buffalo get out of this alive?

Hunkered down in the morning sun, Tom speculated about the men below. He turned to Two Buffalo. "It doesn't make sense. Below, Este Santos has his whole . . . army. He is focused on us and only us. He has to know that the captives are not with us. I would think they would split up, trying to get them back."

"Slaves for work or women to sell for men's entertainment, these can be gotten anywhere. A ride through any village will replace the captives. You and I, my friend, destroyed their supply caves. We embarrassed the jefe. Este Santos wants our bodies hung in his camp for the buzzards to pick at, to remind his men he is still the power in this area."

"We will not escape from this?" Tom concluded.

Two Buffalo leaned back and seemed at peace. "We might not. But, we can learn much about Este Santo. We can watch how he goes about getting to us. It is never too late to gain knowledge. You and I can use it on the other side."

Tom stared at his puzzling friend. To be so comfortable in any situation was to be envied. Tom decided that he was fortunate to die with such a man.

There was movement in the Comancheros' camp. Several men who were hidden in the mound appeared and moved back to the camp. Others took their horses and moved around the east and west edges. Some of the men assembled on the south side, while others rode around to the north side to close off any escape.

Tom watched the men on the east side. One man put something to his eye. It was a telescope or spy glass. Looking at the west side, there was a man doing the same thing. He was able to pick out five men with telescopes, searching the mound for them. It would take very little time for them to find the animals.

"They are spotters for the cannon," Two Buffalo answered the unspoken question. "Others near them are snipers. They may not be able to hit us, but their shots will keep us pinned down for the cannon."

"Is there a next move for us?" Tom asked, picking up the canteen.

"Maybe one. We split up and try and last until dark. Before the moon comes up we will move out on the desert and if it is meant to be, we will survive," he said.

He shook the canteen. It had only a swallow of water left. The coffee last night had helped Tom. There was a shout from below. The man to the east had picked out the animals.

The cannon was turned toward the east side. They watched as the new gunner rammed the powder and ball down.

"It is time. I will see you on the other side," Two Buffalo said, and he aimed the long rifle at the rock wall behind the animals and fired. Rock shards sprayed them, and as one they bolted down the side of the mound. The men moved away from each other, seeking separate cover.

The move with the animals running had been successful. All eyes focused on the running horse and mule, while the two men found places to hide where one cannon ball wouldn't get them both.

Tom knew that remaining still was the best defense. He realized that the canteen was still with him and guilt swept over him. He should have shared it with Two Buffalo. Once again, shouts were heard below.

The gunner moved the cannon and adjusted the elevation. The cannon was touched off and again spewed smoke and fire. Dirt and rock flew in the air from the mound. The bean pot from the night before had been spotted and was now a very dead pot.

A clear miss of the desired targets should have brought a smile, but it was a sobering realization of just how accurate the gunner was with the cannon. Tom scanned the men below, looking for the jefe. He was ready to die. Ironically, at a certain point of the battle a man accepts his fate. He wished for only one more achievement, to get a bullet into Este Santos.

The jefe could be seen directing operations from behind his men. With a lot of luck, Tom could try and put a shot in Santos' direction and hit him. It was further than he had ever tried before, but with some extra powder, maybe. The gunpowder smoke would give him away, but it gave him a goal. If the cannon was aimed in his direction, he would take the shot.

The cannon was loaded and turned to the west of him. Again, it belched smoke and fire. The ball sprayed dirt and rock from the mound. That was in the direction Two Buffalo had gone. He was sure that his friend was well-hidden and the shot was at a false target.

The sun was high and Tom lay still in his cover. He dared not drink from the canteen and show movement for the spotters below. He had seen the paint and Ralph being led to the Comancheros' horses. He was glad they were not shot.

Sweat ran down the sides of Tom's neck and his muscles ached from lack of movement. Through the morning the Comancheros fired the cannon randomly. He knew that their patience would soon run out.

Shouting brought him out of his daydream state. He had been thinking of Eva and of his family in Vermont. Tom wished that he could see them both one more time. Then he would be ready to go with Two Buffalo to the other side.

Below, the Comancheros spread across the three sides of the plateau. They moved as one to the base of the mound. Tom could now hit one with his Hawken rifle. He suddenly realized that that was what they wanted. This was the final push, and some of the men below would be sacrificed.

Once Tom and Two Buffalo were found, the men would move in on them or the cannon would be used to finish them. Tom wouldn't make it easy on them. He decided to stay still until the men were within range of the Colt. He would then empty the revolver on them, maybe even the spare handgun. He would then take a final shot at Este Santos.

The Comancheros started up at the mound. Tom felt relief, knowing that the stalemate would soon be over.

There was another yell from the camp. Tom looked and saw a man pointing to the east. Glancing over, he could see the dust of more riders. That was all he needed, more Comancheros. He saw that all the men had stopped and were watching the dust.

Yips and cries could be heard from the riders. Tom saw the bronzed bodies of the warriors. Their horses had painted markings for war.

"You're too late to attack us," Tom said, his voice raspy from lack of water. "The Comancheros got here first."

"They are here to help," a voice behind him said.

Tom just about jumped out of his skin. Wheeling around, he looked into the wise face of Two Buffalo.

"The warriors are Arapahoe. They are friends to the Cheyenne, but not the Comanche and Comancheros," Two Buffalo explained.

Tom watched as the Comancheros regrouped to face a new threat. The men on the mound ran down, trying to get in position to defend the camp. The gunner swung the cannon around and fired quickly at the approaching Arapahoe. The ball flew long over the charging braves.

He watched as the warriors split, part going for the horses while the rest charged the camp. Gunfire broke out, with both Arapahoe and Comancheros falling. The gunner was trying to load the cannon when the Arapahoe swept down on him. The horses were run off and the camp was overrun.

Comancheros scrambled up the hill to find cover. The spotters and men placed on the north side of the plateau rode hard away from the attack. Tom and Two Buffalo moved down the mound toward the men trying to climb for cover. They emptied their handguns on the Comancheros, driving them back toward the Arapahoe.

Within minutes, the remaining Comancheros were dead or dying. Tom guessed that about half had gotten away. It appeared that one of them was Este Santos. The savagery below continued as the Arapahoe scalped and mutilated the Comancheros. Screaming could be heard when a wounded man was found and scalped. The unfortunate soul would then be blinded and slashed across the limbs and body.

Tom found himself with mixed feelings for the Comancheros. While he believed they deserved death, it should be swift. He watched below as Two Buffalo walked among the Arapahoe introducing himself, and hopefully, telling them to spare his friend Tom.

Each step brought pain to Tom's stiff muscles as he worked his way down the mound. He realized that he was still holding his Colt in his hand. Slipping it into the holster, he continued off the mound. The small cannon lay on its side.

Tom leaned on some large rocks at the base. He knew that he would have to walk out and meet the Arapahoe, but he was not looking forward to seeing the ravaged bodies of the Comancheros.

"Señor, I knew if I waited that the pleasure of killing you would be mine."

Tom looked into the cruel, twisted face of Este Santos, el jefe. He had hidden between the rocks while his men were slaughtered. Now he would achieve his objective, killing the man who had destroyed his caves and humiliated him.

The world was moving in slow motion. Tom watched the jefe's gun come up. He knew that his Colt was empty in the holster. The Hawken rifle was slung on his back, out of reach. At the moment, he couldn't even say if it was loaded or not.

As the jefe's gun lined up on his chest, Tom saw Este Santos' head jerk, blood and tissue bursting from the back. The gun fell from the lifeless hand as his body collapsed into a heap. Tom turned and looked into the eyes of Eva.

Eva slid off the buckskin, dropped the empty rifle to the ground, and came quickly to Tom. She held him so tightly that Tom found it difficult to breathe. She no longer wore the gingham dress. She now had deerskin britches and a long, deerskin shirt.

Stepping back, she looked up at him. "You are not hurt?"

He looked at the black and white streaks of war paint on her cheeks and forehead. She had the blood of a warrior flowing in her veins.

"I am not hurt, Eva," he assured her. "I am tired and very thirsty, and very lucky you were nearby."

Eva handed Tom a water bag and motioned him to follow her. They walked away from the battle area and sat in the shade of a gnarled pine tree.

"After I left with the others, we heard shooting. My heart ached, fearing you would be killed," Eva started. "I knew that getting the others to safely was my responsibility. We came upon this hunting party of Arapahoe."

"One was my uncle. He knew of my father's trade and asked me where my man Samuel was. I told him Samuel was dead and I belonged to another man. I told him you had saved me and were now standing off the Comancheros with a brave Cheyenne, Two Buffalo."

"I asked him to take care of the people with me. I told him that I was going back to die with you."

Tom could see tears in Eva's eyes. What she was telling him was not coming easy.

Eva took a deep breath. "I told him that a warrior would not let someone of his own blood's man be killed without joining the fight."

Tom knew Eva had challenged an elder of the tribe, taking the chance that he would drive her from the camp and wash his hands of the insolent girl.

"My uncle looked in the direction that we had come. He then agreed that the hunt could use more guns and horses. I insisted that he allow me to come."

Two Buffalo came over to Tom and Eva. He was leading the paint and Ralph.

Tom noticed that the strong medicine necklace was gone. "You have lost the necklace?" he asked.

"I gave the necklace to Eva's uncle. I told him that he had done a great deed. He saved my adopted son and the father of my future grandchildren," Two Buffalo replied with a broad smile.

Tom looked at Eva. "You know my future is being a mountain man and the mountains are where I plan to live."

Eva looked into Tom's eyes. "I love the mountains."

Taking her into his arms, he held Eva close. Tom whispered, "I love you. Will you marry me?"

* * *

The group left the slaughter at the mound and rode to meet the rest of the Arapahoe who had not participated in the attack on the Comancheros. They had set up camp in a grove of cottonwoods next to a small stream. There was much excitement as the braves returned with guns, knives, horses, and other spoils of the victory.

That evening the revelry was tempered by the sounds of weeping from those who had lost loved ones in the attack. It was a scene that was played over and over in the Arapahoe camp when the missing braves from a battle were mourned.

Meanwhile, Tom and Eva were basking in the glow of their acknowledged love. After weeks of fear, Eva, finally felt safe. Those around her would now protect her should any of the Comancheros return. Tom officially asked for her hand and the couple talked of their future.

Two Buffalo was in his glory as he told stories of the fight with the Comancheros at the fire each night, entertaining the braves. The uncle proudly displayed the horses and guns that had been collected by the Arapahoe.

Sitting away from the fire, Tom and Eva sat listening to the night sounds when Tom suggested, "We should get married when we're back in Fort William."

"We could be married right here," she replied.

Tom looked at her, confused. "Is your uncle able to marry people?"

"There are two ways we could marry," Eva explained. "The marriage could be arranged by our parents and after sharing a special meal with us and gifts given, we would be married."

"That wouldn't work. My parents are in Vermont," Tom replied, "but I am sure they would be in favor of our marriage."

"Then we will have to run away and live together. Either way, we would be man and wife."

"You don't say vows to each other promising to love, honor, and other things?" he asked.

"Why would we?" she questioned him. "Love is nice but not needed to marry. It is expected that once you are married, you show respect for each other. We are lucky, we do have love."

"We would still get married by a preacher at the fort, right?" he asked.

"Let's ask my uncle and Two Buffalo for advice," Eva said.

The two men were delighted to offer their wisdom. They immediately suggested the special meal. Two Buffalo would act on behalf of Tom and the uncle would represent Eva. The ceremony would be held the very next day. They had ample supplies for a celebration taken from the Comancheros.

Upon hearing of the marriage, the Arapahoe women ushered Eva away, insisting that the two not see each other until the ceremony. Some of the Arapahoe braves offered to build a wedding lodge for the couple.

The next day Tom wandered around the camp like a lost soul. He had bathed in the cool of the morning, the soothing stream water flowing around him. He found a small mirror and scissors in the Comancheros' supplies and carefully trimmed his hair and beard. He put on his spare trousers and wool shirt.

Twice during the day, he caught a glimpse of Eva. Once when the women were taking her to bathe, and again at the cook fire, which he was not allowed to go near. Two Buffalo was dressed in new buckskin trousers and a cape that was decorated with quills and beads. He and Tom spent most of the afternoon together to help pass the time until the ceremony.

Finally, it was time. Tom was surprised at how nervous he felt. As he and Two Buffalo walked toward the ceremonial fire, he had nervous flutters in his stomach and his legs were shaking. They had the two spare cap and ball revolvers as a gift to Eva's uncle. To help keep his mind off the coming events, Tom had cleaned them until they shined.

Two Buffalo had donned a headdress befitting of a Cheyenne chief. He walked proudly beside Tom. Suddenly, Eva stepped out of the group near the fire. Tom's breath caught as he saw her, dressed in a decorated doeskin dress. Her hair and shoulders were adorned in wild flowers, framing the beauty of her face.

As though numb, Tom stood through the short ceremony. From his first glimpse of Eva to this moment flashed through his mind. He couldn't believe that the two of them would be together from now on. Only Two Buffalo and the uncle said any words. Finally, the uncle said something in Arapahoe to Eva and she stepped forward, reaching her hand out to Tom. As he took her hand, he whispered, "I do."

The rest of the Arapahoe broke into a shrill chorus of delight as they crowded around the couple, several reaching out and touching them, to share their strong medicine. Tom pulled Eva close and kissed her to the cheers of the crowd.

The uncle led the way to prepared meal. After everyone was seated on the buffalo hides spread about, he lit a ceremonial pipe and shared it with Tom and Two Buffalo, confirming that there would be peace between the parties present. Concluding the ceremonial events, everyone dug into the meal. Tom ate and smiled, but he didn't taste anything. His only thoughts were when he and Eva would finally be alone.

There were songs, chanting, and dancing around the fire. Bottles of whiskey were opened and the celebration went until well after midnight. Finally, Tom felt it was acceptable to bid the uncle and Two Buffalo good night. Leaving the others to the merriment, the couple made their way to the lodge. The floor was covered with furs and the fire outside created soft light through the hastily built lodge walls.

Tom and Eva stood in the middle of the lodge. She undid the ties on her dress and it slipped to the floor, exposing her soft, naked skin. She sat and watched as Tom hurried to remove his clothing. She lay back, her arms reaching as he joined her.

CHAPTER FIFTEEN

It was full daylight when Tom awoke. Shafts of sunlight pierced the dim interior of the lodge. He looked into the dark, smiling eyes of his Arapahoe wife. "How are you this morning, my husband?"

"I wish we could lie here forever, but nature and thirst force me to get up," he said, holding Eva close for a moment.

She watched as he pulled on his clothes. Eva could not remember feeling so happy for a very long time. The bright light caused her to squint as he opened the flap to exit the lodge.

Many of the braves lay where they had fallen after too much to drink the night before. There was a wisp of smoke from the dying coals of the celebration fire. Tom walked into the cottonwoods and relieved himself. On the way back, he knelt at the stream and drank before washing his face to clear the cobwebs.

Returning with some wood, Tom soon had a fire going. Two Buffalo was nowhere to be seen.

Searching through the packs, Tom found the coffee and put on a pot of water to heat. Footsteps behind him let him know that Eva had come from the lodge.

"You didn't come back," she said, pretending to pout.

Tom stammered a moment, trying to explain that he was making her some coffee, but before he could complete what he was trying to say, she came close and kissed him. "I've got to wash."

She ran her fingers across his broad back before heading for the stream to bathe. Tom sat waiting for the water to boil, deep in thought. He had not expected to survive the attack of the Comancheros and had thought little of the future. For the first time his thoughts went beyond the return to Fort William.

He had his cache at the Green River rendezvous site. He needed to make a trip to retrieve his gear. He would go through the South Pass, and he could inquire about Chess at the small trading post located there.

Freshly bathed, Eva brought him a cup and filled it with coffee. She then began to put together breakfast for them. It was unlikely that the other braves would wake anytime soon. The sound of riders brought their attention to the south. It was Two Buffalo and her uncle.

Seeing the two coming, Eva added more to the meal. Carrying his cup, Tom walked to meet the men. Smiling, Two Buffalo called out, "I didn't expect to see you before midday."

"I see you were up early," Tom replied, ignoring the kidding. "I take it you went back to the mound."

"We surprised a couple of the Comancheros that had come back looking for anything of value," Two Buffalo said. "They now sleep with the others."

Tom saw the bloody scalps hanging from the saddle of Eva's uncle. When he returned to the fire, the meal was ready. Eva filled the men's plates before taking some for herself. She had mixed cold flour with water and the resulting porridge was warm and satisfying.

Finishing his plate, Tom said, "It is time that we head back for Fort William. There is much to do before this winter's trapping."

Eva looked up from her meal. She smiled at her husband, but there was a shadow of worry on her face. "We can leave tomorrow," she agreed. "My uncle and his people will be returning to their hunt."

There was much to do before they could leave. Tom and Two Buffalo returned to the mound. The sounds and smells of the area were similar to the plain after a buffalo hunt, except the carcasses lying on the bloody grass were men. The bodies of the Arapahoe who had been killed had been removed for burial, but the Comancheros lay where they had fallen, bloated and covered with flies.

The smell of death was heavy in the air. Tom avoided looking at them as best he could. He planned to use a cart and two of the Comancheros' oxen to haul things back to the fort. The small cannon was one of the first things loaded onto the cart. It would bring a fair price at the fort. A few other items that didn't suit the itinerant life of the Arapahoe had been left and these, too, he loaded.

Tom was thankful to leave the carnage of the mound. He vowed that he would never return to the spot. He drove the cart with his buckskin tied to the back. Soon he would have to tell Eva of his plans to return to the Green River for the cache. He wanted her to stay in the safety of the fort and wasn't sure how she would react to his request.

After one more night in the wedding lodge, Tom and Eva with Two Buffalo headed north for the fort. Tom tied Ralph and the buckskin to the back of the cart and sat in its seat with Eva. The lumbering oxen could only travel 15 miles a day. Two Buffalo ranged out in front of them, hunting and watching for trouble. It would take almost two weeks travel across the sun-drenched plain to arrive back at Fort William, making for a hot and dusty honeymoon.

The stockade wall came into view at the confluence of the Laramie and North Platte River. It was late in the day, so the group decided to camp on the east side of the Laramie River for the night. Two Buffalo had shot a small deer, giving them venison for their supper.

While Eva skinned the young buck, Tom picketed the animals. The oxen were in very good condition and would give them additional money. The cart needed work and could be abandoned if it didn't sell. By the time he had finished with the animals he caught the smell of broiling steaks.

The sun was starting to go down and lights from the fort could be seen. The sounds of celebrating soldiers or trappers drifted across the river. Tom would have to find a place for Eva to stay while he went to get his cache. He hoped that Louie could help him with that. Two Buffalo had told him that in a couple of days he planned to ride back to his village and spend time with his people.

Before heading back to the Green River, Tom wanted to get married by some official at the fort. While he felt as committed as he could to Eva, his Protestant upbringing pushed him to commit to each other with vows. Eva fully supported his request.

Louie welcomed them with a broad smile the next day. The mid-summer heat baked the dusty compound. Tom and Eva had bathed early that morning but blowing dust and sweat had already left their faces streaked.

While Eva looked for a few things she would need, Tom stood at the counter with Louie. "Isn't that the woman the old geezer bought from her father?" he asked.

"It is," Tom replied. "The old fellow was killed and she was taken to be sold in Mexico. After some doing, I got her back."

"That's right, I remember he was taking her to the rendezvous," Louie recalled.

"We want to get married," Tom said.

Louie looked at his friend with doubt on his face. "There's not a preacher that would marry you and an Indian here at the fort."

Disappointed, Tom asked, "Do you know where we could get married?"

Smiling, Louie told him, "I can do it for you. I'm not a clergy but it will be legal."

It was settled. That evening, at the Buffalo Hide Saloon, Louie had the ceremony in one of the back rooms. As a gift to Tom and Eva, he put on a nice spread for the guests to dine on. Two Buffalo sat with the wedding party as the honorary father of the bride.

That night, over mugs of a good, stout beer, Louie told Tom that he could use some help at the post, and if Eva wanted to work he would include a small room for her. Tom wanted to wait to tell Eva. Tonight, he didn't want her thinking about his leaving. After the wedding party, he and Eva were Louie's guest in the boarding house.

The couple awoke early and lay in bed, talking. Knowing that he couldn't put it off any longer, Tom told her about having to go to the Green River.

"I am ready to go when you are," she told him.

Tom was suddenly silent and he tried to come up with what to say next. Noticing this, Eva asked, "I won't be going?"

"I want you to stay here, in the safety of the fort," he told her.

Eva sat up on the edge of the bed, the covers falling from her naked shoulders. "You want me to stay here and do nothing while I worry if you would come back safely?" she asked.

"Louie needs help and you could work for him until I get back," Tom said, the suggestion sounding lame.

She turned to him on the bed, tears welling up in her eyes. "I can help you on your trip."

Putting his arm around her, he pulled her closer. "I will only be gone for three or four weeks." He felt a tear splash onto his arm.

Something he hadn't even considered during the quest to get Eva had been the fact that once they were together, the life he longed for would require him to leave her alone for long periods of time.

Tom searched his mind for the words that would make her understand his concern for her being safe in the fort. He even started to wonder if it would be okay for her to come, when Eva whispered, "I will be waiting for you, Tom Franklin."

The rest of the day, with Eva's help, Tom got his supplies together for the trip. He felt a sense of guilt leaving his new wife so soon. Eva began to talk about the wedding the night before. It helped to cut the tension and bring the two of them back into good spirits.

Two Buffalo stopped by and told Tom that he would be leaving for his village, promising to be back about the same time as Tom.

With everything ready, Tom planned an early departure the next morning. He and Eva walked along the river and enjoyed the coolness of the evening. Tom talked of growing up in Vermont and of losing his brother Isaac on the Ohio River. They stopped and sat on a bench that someone had placed under a willow. The breeze rippled the new gingham dress she was wearing. Her hair was in a loose braid on her back.

Tom sat in the moment, finding it hard to believe that the beautiful woman beside him was now his wife. Eva rubbed her hand along his broad back and teased the hair on the back of his neck, sending pleasant chills through him. Tom promised himself that when he got back, he would find his wife a proper home, a home she would be comfortable in, and he could come back to.

Louie had purchased the small cannon and traded a mustang for the oxen. With the horse, Tom could use the mule for a pack animal. He wanted to leave the buckskin with Eva. Her few items had been moved from the boarding house to the room in the back of the trading post. The couple had a late supper before spending the last night in the boarding house. Try as they might, neither got much sleep that night.

Clouds had come in overnight and the morning air was still. There were flashes of heat lightning in the distance. Tom leaned over the bed and kissed Eva, promising to be back as soon as he could. She clung to him briefly before releasing him and lying back down.

The small lamp gave feeble light at the livery door. Taking it from the hook to cut the inky darkness of the building, Tom headed toward the back to ready the mustang and mule. The mule was outfitted with a sawbuck saddle to tie his packs. Once the mustang was saddled, he shoved the Hawken in the scabbard. His Colt was on his right and the skinning knife on his left. He had his light wool shirt open in the front. Two Buffalo had given him a new, flat-brimmed leather hat for a wedding gift.

Riding out of the livery, leading the mule, Tom hung the lantern back on its peg. He would follow the North Platte River to the Sweetwater River to get to the South Pass. Riding past the boarding house, he missed seeing Eva standing in the shadows. "Be safe, dear husband," she whispered.

Chewing on a biscuit, Tom rode west along the river. It felt exhilarating to be back on the trail. In a matter of days, he would be back in the mountains. He looked forward to seeing the rendezvous site again. He knew that he should be feeling guilt about leaving his wife behind, but the lure of the mountains was strong.

It was the last of July and the grass would soon turn from the shades of blue green to gold. On the way to the South Pass, Tom would be climbing in elevation and the taller grass of the plain would give way to the shorter grass and sage brush of the high plain. With good weather and steady riding, Tom expected to reach the cache in 10 days.

Riding alone on the plain, Tom tried to keep to lower ground. He had to remain alert to danger at all times. Toward evening he looked for a place to camp that gave him some cover. His fire was kept small to avoid drawing attention.

The sounds of the night animals were familiar to Tom and he poured his last cup of coffee and doused his fire. The heavy cloud cover had remained and had given an impressive display of reds and oranges at sunset. Someplace to his south there was the grunting of buffalo as they slowly worked their way past in the darkness.

The lack of sleep the night before and the long ride sent Tom to his blankets shortly after his meal. Using his saddle for a pillow and his Colt underneath it, he laid the Hawken just under the edge of his blanket, he was soon in a deep sleep.

It was full light when Tom woke. He felt a flash of panic, unsure for the moment of where he was. As he became aware, Tom realized that he had slept far too soundly. Sitting up, he looked to the west and saw a wall of slowly moving buffalo. "Damn," he mumbled, "I'll lose time today."

After a light breakfast of coffee and hard bread, Tom followed the slow-moving herd for three hours. The wooly beasts would drink from the Platte and then slowly move back onto the plain. It was late morning when the herd moved away from the river, allowing enough room to ride past.

Tom spurred the mustang on and rode at a trot for the next two miles before he came to the far side of the herd. In the south he saw flashes of heat lightning. Tom wanted to put distance between himself and the herd in case the storm came his way. Thunder could start the buffalo running and cause him to flee for his life in front of them.

Wanting to make up for the time lost, Tom rode until darkness started to set in. All of a sudden, he pulled the mustang to a stop. Ahead of him, next to some boulders, was a mounted Indian watching him. He could barely make the rider out in the low light. Suddenly, whatever he saw disappeared.

Tom wondered if his eyes had played tricks on him. There was always the chance of hostiles looking for horses and guns. Removing the loop off his Colt, Tom then pulled the Hawken from the scabbard.

The cluster of boulders were less than a quarter-mile above the river. Tom figured that if he passed within the shadows along the bank, he could get by without being seen. Moving along the river as quietly as possible, Tom rode slumped in the saddle to lower his profile. Ralph, being led behind him, was taking exception to traveling along the river and began to pull on the lead rope, wanting to go back to the trail.

Tom rode with his heart in his throat, wanting to, but not daring to, scold the mule, and fearing it would start braying anytime, giving them away. Finally, he was forced to dismount and take the mule's lead rope short.

"Stop this damn stuff, you stubborn cuss," he hissed at the animal.

"Maybe it is ready to stop for the night," a voice behind him said.

The surprise of someone speaking did everything but make Tom wet himself as he stumbled under the mule's neck, putting it between him and the speaker. As quickly as he was startled, he became relieved. It was Two Buffalo!

"Don't do that!" Tom exclaimed. "You scared me out of ten years of my life!"

Smirking, Two Buffalo replied, "I sat on my horse until I was sure you saw me."

Climbing out from behind the mule, Tom said, "Sure, I saw something, but I sure as heck didn't know it was you. How did you know it was me?"

"I recognized the fine, new hat I bought you," he answered as he turned away. "I have coffee on and two birds roasting. You may as well wash up in the river before coming up."

Feeling more foolish than upset, Tom led the animals into the camp. He still felt it necessary to explain himself. "You were supposed to go to your village."

"The birds are almost done. Get me some biscuits from my pack and I'll warm them," Two Buffalo said, then added, "The coffee is ready."

Tom brought the sack of biscuits to his friend and then filled two cups with coffee. Sitting against a boulder, he tasted the hot brew. "What happened to going to see your people?" he repeated.

"I was packed and ready to leave," he told Tom. "I stopped to say goodbye to Eva. A sadder soul I had never seen. She worried she would never see you again. I asked her if it would help if I was with you. She put her arms around me and said yes."

"She didn't trust that I could take care of myself?" Tom asked, feeling slighted.

"Eva knows the man you are. In a fight, there is no one braver. It would be the not knowing of what happened to you that would be painful to live with," he replied. "With me here, she would know that if something bad happened, you would not be alone."

Tom knew that everyone meant well, but his feathers had been ruffled. While he didn't say it, he was happy to have company on the trip. He was glad when the birds were done and they started enjoying the tender meat.

After a mouthful, Tom asked, "How did you get ahead of me?"

"I rode up the north side of the river," Two Buffalo replied. "This morning I saw you were stuck behind the buffalo and knew you would need a hot meal."

"Yes, the damn buffalo," Tom remembered. The food and his friend were raising his spirits. "It is a tasty meal."

The men headed west, thankful that they weren't being chased by anyone on this trip. Their conversation remained light, avoiding the confrontation with the Comancheros. The clouds were gone, the sun was bright and the sky seemed to go on forever across the endless plain. Puffy clouds floated above, giving them brief periods of shade.

The men were four days from the South Pass when they reached Independence Rock. They had been climbing in elevation and would continue to do so the rest of the way to the pass. The grass had gotten thinner and the dark sagebrush dotted the plain. After setting up camp near the base, Tom climbed part-way up the face, looking at all the names that had been chiseled into the granite. Using the back of his hatchet, he put his name and the date into the stone.

Climbing down, he looked up at the 130 foot-high rounded top. Two Buffalo came up beside him. "Your name will tell people of your passing for all time. They will stop and ask, who was Tom Franklin?"

"Someday I will bring Eva here and let her add her name next to mine," Tom replied.

Shaking his head, Two Buffalo walked back to the camp. "A good life is one that lives in the memories of men and leaves no mark on the land."

"Well, right now I am ready to put some teeth marks in our supper," Tom said, chuckling.

They were using dried buffalo droppings for their fire. The fuel burned hot and clean, but did not last long. The two men chose to drink tea with the meal of fried side meat and rice. While eating, Tom thought about the coming winter's trapping. Tom hoped to learn more about the Wind River region at the South Pass trading post.

The next three days were clear and hot. Tom brought down a pronghorn, giving them some fresh meat for the evening meals. It had fed on sage, so the meat had the smell and taste of the brush. Once the sun went down the high desert gave up the day's warmth.

Lying under his blankets, Tom watched the night sky. Every so often he would see a star streak across the sky. As a child, his mother had told him to make a wish on a fallen star and it would come true. Right now, Tom wished that Eva was with him.

They got an early start the next morning. Steam from the animals' breath hung in the air as they headed west. The two men talked about reaching the trading post. Tom wondered if there would be any word from Chess. For all he knew, his bay might be there.

Alarm went through Tom as he saw smoke rising in the sky. His first thought was a grass fire, which could be deadly. "It is not a grass fire," Two Buffalo replied. "I think there has been trouble at the trading post." They watched the smoke for miles as they rode toward the trading post. The building was charred ruins by the time they got there.

Two men lay in the dirt in front of the post. Tom stopped short of the area and dismounted, ground reining the mustang. Two Buffalo rode in a circle around the area, looking for sign. The bloody wounds of the bodies were covered with flies. Both men had been scalped. Tom turned to get the mustang and mule when he heard a groan. One of the men was still alive!

The younger of the two men was barely breathing. As Tom approached the man groaned again. Kneeling next to the wounded man, he rolled him onto his back, using a hat lying nearby to support the head. The man was bloodied everywhere, making it impossible to tell how many times he had been wounded.

Taking a moment, Tom check the second man to see if there was any life. He had already begun to stiffen in death. Two Buffalo rode up and seeing that Tom was working on one of the men, slid from the paint and came to help.

They moved the wounded man to the shade of some small bushes upwind of the smoldering trading post. Evidence of a stomach wound gave little hope of the man surviving, even if it was the only one. Two Buffalo gathered coals from the building and had put water to heat.

Finishing cleaning the injuries the best he could, Tom covered the man with one of the blankets from the bedroll on the mustang to keep the flies off. He was about to go and move the other body when he noticed that the wounded man's eyes were open.

"Water . . . water," the young man whispered.

Taking his canteen, he poured some in the cap and gave it to the man. The wounded man began to cough as he tried to swallow. Taking his time, Tom was able to get some water down the man.

Barely audible, the young man whispered, "Where is my pa?"

Tom glanced back toward the body still lying in front of the building. "He didn't make it, son."

The wounded man grabbed Tom's arm, "Promise . . . promise you will bury him," the boy begged, the effort to cling to Tom's arm becoming too much, his hand fell to his side.

For a moment, Tom thought the wounded man had died, but he continued the shallow breathing. Two Buffalo came from a small shed that had been spared the fire. He had a shovel and set it next to the bushes.

"I'll take that and get his father under the ground," Tom said.

The dirt near the cabin was rocky. For an hour Tom labored before he had a hole deep enough to bury the young man's father. Leaving the shovel near the grave, he went to get the body.

"We will need another hole," Two Buffalo said.

Tom looked at the still form of the young man. He almost felt a sense of relief knowing that the boy's suffering was over. Red streaks from the setting sun were in the sky by the time both bodies were buried. Tom stood with his hat in hand and said words over the father and son.

Leaving the graves, Tom walked to the small stream behind the burnt post to wash off the blood and sweat. He sat, exhausted from the labors and stress of the day. He heard Two Buffalo coming up behind him. His friend set a cup of coffee on the ground next to him.

"I wish we knew their names," Tom said.

"They are together on the other side," Two Buffalo said. "Names will no longer be important. They will have each other and those that went before them."

Walking back to the fire, Tom saw that his friend had a haunch of the antelope roasting over the fire. He suddenly realized that he hadn't eaten all day. "I hope the meat's almost done, I'm starving."

While they chewed slivers of meat from the haunch, Two Buffalo told his friend, "The boy spoke of prisoners before he died."

"Prisoners?" Tom asked.

"He said it was Crow that had attacked and they had taken two trappers with them," the chief said. "I found tracks coming in from the west and leaving toward the north. Maybe ten braves."

"The Crow haven't been causing trouble," Tom said.

"They are pushed by other tribes with more horses and guns. They may have come for both from this trading post," Two Buffalo guessed.

"We are headed north to the Green River to get my cache," Tom said. "We might be their next target."

Finishing cutting the last of his meat off the antelope bone, Tom tossed it into the fire. He thought about the two trappers who had been taken by the Crow. Whether they lived or died would be at the whim of the leader. While no guns were found near the bodies, the father and son had probably been caught away from the post and had died in a running battle trying to get back inside. For some reason the trappers hadn't gotten into the fight, or they too would have been killed.

The sun was just coming up when the two men rode away from the burned trading post. For most of the morning they followed the Crows' tracks. Two Buffalo pointed out the tracks of two horses being led. They would be the ones with the trappers. Other horses were being driven in front of the braves.

Common sense told Tom that they should be putting distance between the Crow and themselves. As much as he might have wanted to, he couldn't just ride away and leave the two trappers. It was unlikely that he and the chief's pursuit would spare the lives of the men, but at least they could bury whatever was left after the braves tired of abusing them.

All of a sudden, Two Buffalo held up his hand, warning Tom to stop. The chief swung off the paint and pointed. "The Crow have split up. The horses being driven have been pushed toward the east. The rest are continuing toward the Popo Agie River.

"We will follow the braves driving the horses," the chief said. "The others are headed for the Crows' summer camp."

"Why would they drive the horses away from their camp?" Tom asked.

"Grazing is poor near the river," Two Buffalo explained. "The young braves will watch the extra horses in one of the valleys nearby."

"Shouldn't we head for the trappers at the Crows' camp?"

"First, we will locate their horses, and then we will find their camp. We may be able to drive some of the horses away and we will have less men chasing us," the old chief said.

An hour later, the two lay on a ridge overlooking the Crow horses grazing on the valley floor. Tom was focused on a bay that looked much like the one he'd had stolen. Near the mouth of the valley, four braves sat near a small fire. High on the valley walls were two other Crow standing watch. In the distance they could see smoke from the camp on Popo Agie.

There was another hour of daylight. Two of the braves near the fire mounted their horse and rode toward the main camp. "The braves below have bows to defend the horses," Two Buffalo said. "Soon the Crow on the walls will come down for their meal. They won't go back up until after daylight tomorrow."

"I think the bay below is the horse I had taken at the rendezvous," Tom told his friend.

"It has the marks of the wolves that attacked it last winter," Two Buffalo said. "I am sure it is yours. Now, we must go and find the Crow camp."

They worked their way back off the ridge and to the animals. They rode west beyond a rise before heading north, skirting around the valley opening. Tom's stomach was tight as they rode toward the camp. He expected an arrow to strike him at any time.

They dismounted and tied the horses and mule well away from the Crow camp. Tom wondered if they had just delivered more stock to the Crow. If things went badly, they would most likely be killed.

The shouts of men rose from the camp. "They're celebrating the victory at the trading post," the chief whispered.

"If the men are dead, we should go for the horses and leave," Tom told his friend.

Without answering, Two Buffalo continued to work his way through the boulders toward the river. The Crow camp came into view, several hundred paces away. There were teepees spread across both sides of the river. A large fire burned in the center, near the river. Women and children sat just beyond the firelight, watching the men.

Dusk had settled in and the light from the flames showed the two trappers' naked bodies hanging from a wooden frame, their wrists tied to the horizontal upper pole. They hung, their bodies limp. Tom feared that they were too late.

One of the braves dancing around the fire and waved a stick with glowing brands on the tip. He poked each of the prisoners, causing them to flinch. The men were still alive. Tom crouched, watching the scene in front of them. He didn't see any way that they could get in and rescue the men. He almost wished that they had found them dead, so the torture would be over.

Looking over at Two Buffalo, he saw that the chief had settled in for a wait. With a feeling of helplessness, Tom watched the horrific spectacle in the camp. The dancing Crow waved whiskey bottles gotten from the trading post along with glowing sticks over their heads as they danced.

Tom clutched the Hawken rifle. He had decided that if the braves attempted to go at either of the trappers with a knife, he would use it to kill the Crow and then pull the Colt.

As the night progressed, a Crow brave would stumble to the side and collapse onto the animal hides spread around. Suddenly, Tom began to see the strategy that Two Buffalo was using. He was waiting until the braves had drunk themselves into a stupor and then go in after the trappers.

After several hours of celebrating, the women and children had retired to their teepees. Finally, the last dancer staggered by the prisoners, swinging a stick viciously across their bodies. The trappers barely moved, being nearly unconscious. Two Buffalo waited until the fire had burned down, leaving the trappers in darkness. Snores and coughing were heard from the sleeping braves.

Two Buffalo touched his friend's shoulder, startling him. Tom had begun to doze from the hours of waiting. "You go in and cut down the trappers," the chief whispered. "I will bring in the horses."

"Horses?" Tom asked.

"They will be too heavy to carry out," his friend replied.

Tom moved out of their hiding place, his cramped leg muscles protesting. There were several teepees between him and the fire. Doing the best stalking of his life, he went noiselessly past, approaching the men from behind.

In a hoarse whisper, he said, "If you are awake, don't make a sound." Neither of the men reacted to his voice.

Setting his Hawken against the upright, he pulled his skinning knife and cut the bonds of the first man, lowering the unconscious man to the ground. He then cut the first wrist of the second man loose.

Grabbing around his waist, he cut the second bond, the man's arm falling limp.

There was a slight sound behind him. Tom froze, holding his breathe. "Let me help you." It was Two Buffalo. Together they lifted the man Tom was holding and draped him over the mustang's saddle.

Expecting the Crow to erupt around him at any moment, Tom put the other man onto the paint with Two Buffalo's help. Taking his Hawken, he joined the chief leading the horses away from the camp. When they reached the mule, they lowered the men from the horses and attempted to wake them.

Tom tried to give the trappers water from his canteen. One of the men gagged, barely getting a swallow. The other grabbed at the canteen, wanting more water. "Take it easy," Tom warned. "I need you to sit on the horse."

In the darkness, they got the conscious man onto the paint. Tom pulled his coat off the back of his saddle and helped the man put it over his shoulders. He then sat on the mustang, holding the disoriented trapper in front of him. Two Buffalo tied the mule's lead rope to the paint's saddle. "Ride west to the mountains," he said. "I know a pass that will take us to the Green River. Light a fire just before the sun comes up and I will find you."

Tom wanted to object about leaving Two Buffalo behind, but he knew it was best to follow the wise old chief's instructions. The mountains to the west were called the Wind River Range and were about 10 miles away. Thankful that they had gotten the men out of the Crow camp, he put the North Star on his left and headed west.

A couple of hours before sunup, he reached the foothills of the mountains. Stopping next to a stand of red pine, Tom almost dropped the man as he struggled to get the trapper in front of him to the ground. The only thing that told him the trapper was still alive were the groans emitted every time he moved him.

The man on the paint was able to dismount under his own power. Tom spread a blanket over the trapper he had helped off the horse. After offering a little more water to both of the men, he then began looking for wood for the fire. The trapper from the paint had pulled Two Buffalo's bedroll from the saddle and sat with the blanket wrapped around him.

They had passed a small stream before getting to the pines, so Tom took a pot and filled it along with the coffee pot. Figuring that it was time to start the fire, he struck his flint with the back of his skinning knife, sending a shower of sparks into some tinder. Soon he had the small fire going and put the pots of water next to the flames to heat.

"Tom," a weak voice said. "Is that you?"

Looking at the man he had laid onto the ground, he replied, "Yes, my name is Tom."

"It's me . . . Chess."

A flash went through Tom's body. One of the trappers they had saved was Chess! "How the hell did the Crow get you?"

"It were our own damn fault," Chess said, propping himself up with his elbow. "Me and Avery here, was dead drunk when the Crow attack."

Tom could see the tears in Chess' eyes in the firelight. "I deserved everything the Crow done to me. They come in and killed Rene and his boy, and I didn't lift a finger to help."

"It wasn't your doing that caused the death of the man and his boy," Tom said. "If you had been in the fight, you might have gotten one or two, but we would have found you dead and scalped, right along with the others."

For the next hour, Tom cleaned and dressed the wounds of the two men as best he could. Digging extra clothes from the saddle bags, he found enough for the men to wear. They would remain barefooted.

The sun was just coming up when Two Buffalo rode up on Chess' buckskin, leading a sorrel and Tom's bay. Tom noticed that there were saddles and saddle bags on the buckskin and sorrel. The chief swung down. Tom took the horses and tied them to the lower pine branches.

Chess and Avery were sitting at the fire with cups of coffee. Both men looked concerned before they realized that Two Buffalo was a friend. Smiling, the chief said, "You men are looking much better than when we found you."

"The big fellow is Avery," Tom told the chief. "The other fellow is Chess. He was the fellow I went to the rendezvous with."

Filling a cup, Two Buffalo took a drink and then said, "I scattered the horses from the valley. The Crow will be delayed a short time. We need to start across the mountains."

While switching his saddle to the bay, Tom asked, "Where did you get the saddles?"

"The Crow had the horses and gear in their camp. The guns were gone, but the saddle bags were still full," Two Buffalo explained. "I saw them when we went to get the men. I went back and got the horses and gear, and then used them to get the bay."

A half-hour after the chief had arrived the men started over the mountains. With Two Buffalo leading the way, they headed up the narrow trail that led across narrow ledges on the towering peaks. Tom brought up the rear, his stirrup scraping the granite wall beside him and a several hundred-foot drop on the other side.

Chess rode with his head down and his eyes closed as he clung to the saddle horn. Avery had a devil-may-care attitude and seemed to enjoy looking down into the ravine beside them. Looking back before the plain behind them disappeared, Tom saw the Crow braves riding hard toward the mountains.

They had a two-hour lead on the Crow and the braves might decide against coming over the mountains. They would gain little by engaging Tom and his group in a fight on the narrow paths. Tom was glad when the plain behind them was lost beyond the mountains. The reached a small, grassy flat near midday.

Tom pulled wood off some scrub trees and made some coffee. The trappers were unable to stand and sat, exhausted from the ride and their ordeal. Sitting next to Chess, Tom said, "We got about four more hours according to the chief. Then we'll be in a long valley that is a day's ride from the Green River."

"I wish the hell I had more energy," Chess said. "I got quite a crack on the noggin when I tried to make a break from the Crow."

"You're doing just fine, Chess," Tom replied. "I'll heat up some cold flour and water so you have something hot in your stomach."

They let the trappers rest for an hour and eat their fill before moving out. Avery dug some moccasins from his saddle bags that Two Buffalo had retrieved. Both men had been severely sunburned and the clothing was painful against their skin. With his jaw set, Chess followed Two Buffalo across the next pass.

CHAPTER SIXTEEN

Throughout the rest of the day the men worked their way across the mountains. Several times they had to lead the animals. Chess wore two pairs of woolen socks to protect his feet from the sharp rocks. At one point they came face to face with a grizzly bear on one of the narrow passes. Tom worked his way to the front and stood ready with the Hawken. He would get only one shot with the rifle, and if the bear was wounded and charged it would send them all over the side of the trail and down to their deaths in the ravine.

The horses stomped and snorted, fearful of the large silver tip blocking their trail. The mustang attempted to turn around and run when it went over the side of the trail, tumbling down the steep side, screaming until it smashed onto the rocks at the bottom. Two Buffalo and the trappers held tight to the other animals to prevent them from following the mustang.

Tom didn't dare to look back at the tragedy, fearful to take his eyes off the grizzly. The bear stood roaring at the group in his way. Any other place, Tom would have shot the large bear for its hide and claws, but not on a ledge with no way to turn. After what seemed like an eternity, the bear decided that the route was not that important, reversed direction and disappeared.

The men led their animals along the trail. The smell of the bear was strong and the mule began to bray loudly. "Damn you, Ralph!" Tom hollered. "My nerves are worn enough, without you getting on them."

The sun was low as the men rode down the steep path toward the long valley. The men squinted against the glare of the sun. Tom led the mule and was forced to drop the lead rope and the animals slid on their haunches on a talus slope near the base of the trail. In a cloud of dust and sliding rock the men and animals reached the bottom.

The mule stood a distance from the bottom and watched the others ride out of the dust. Tom didn't try to get the lead rope. He knew that Ralph would continue to follow them to wherever they camped for the night. Once in the valley, darkness came quickly. They stopped near a small waterfall to make camp. Tom picketed the animals on the thick grass on the valley floor while Two Buffalo got a fire together. Avery helped collect wood while Chess sat, too tired to move.

That evening Tom cut thick slices of side meat into the frying pan. While they snapped and sputtered, he added coffee to the steaming water. Chess was starting to move around, having rested while camp was set up.

Sitting next to the fire, soaking hard bread into the side meat grease, Tom observed, "Chess, I'm glad to see you're feeling better."

"It's the damn headache," Chess explained. "I could feel every step of the buckskin."

"Where were you and Avery headed?"

"After you left the rendezvous, Avery here moved in the teepee with me. We decided to head down the river to Fort Davy Crockett, after things were over. We got there just in time to see them closing the fort down. The spring rains had left the place a mess. We did a little hunting in the area and looked for a good spot to trap beaver for the coming season. We had no luck and headed back north. We were heading for Fort Hall." Chess took a long drink of coffee before continuing.

"We got to South Pass with a powerful thirst and got us a couple of bottles. We set up camp behind the post near the creek. Rene and his boy joined us after supper, bringing some more rye. We was having a fine time telling stories. I don't recall when they left. The whiskey must have taken over. The next thing I knew, something was poking me in the back. I opened my eyes and there stood a Crow holding a spear. I tried to move toward my rifle, but they were all around us. That was when I got hit on the head."

Chess sat quietly for a moment, his coffee forgotten. "They wanted to keep us for fun later. We were trussed up and put on our horses. I could see Rene and the boy, covered with blood in the yard. It wasn't right, us surviving and them dead."

The fire had burned down and Tom went to check on the animals. It was probably good for Chess to talk about the trading post, but Tom missed the happy-go-lucky man he had met on the way to the rendezvous.

The next morning the group rode along the valley, heading west to the Green River Rendezvous site. Unless the Crow came over the mountain, there was no way that they could ride south around the range and get there first. Two Buffalo figured that they would watch for them in the South Pass area.

Coming to the site of the rendezvous, Tom stood in the stirrups of the bay and looked over the area. Not much was left from the hundreds of men who had attended. He smiled, seeing the rundown teepee still standing. There were a few odds and ends half-hidden in the grass. A cart with a broken wheel had been abandoned near the river. The summer rains had healed most of the scars from the gathering.

The men set up camp near the teepee. The cache was about a mile away, near some red stone cliffs. Tom would retrieve the items tomorrow. He sat near their fire and thought back to the excitement that had been here earlier this summer. He couldn't believe that it would be the last rendezvous.

Chess stood looking toward the area where the tents had been erected. "Talk was that this rendezvous wouldn't be. I must admit that the number of beaver pelts were down this year and the prices even worse. When Bridger left, he figured it was the end. Most trappers are bringing their furs and buying supplies at the forts."

Despite talking of this rendezvous' being the last, returning to the Green River had improved Chess' mood. Tom was seeing the man he had met in June. Part of the cache was a pair of calf-high moccasins. When retrieving his gear, Tom gave these to the trapper. There was also a muzzle loader that had been won in a shooting contest. It was the older style and hadn't been converted to percussion caps. This too, Tom gave to Chess, along with some powder and balls.

Two days later, Tom and Two Buffalo waved good bye to the trappers. Chess promised to look them up at Fort William in the future and pay them back. The mule was loaded with traps and other gear that would be needed for the coming winter's season. Tom had come up with a plan and was anxious to get back to the fort and share it with Eva.

They camped the second night just shy of the South Pass. To prevent being exposed in the broad basin of the Green River, they took the more difficult route along the western foot hills of the Wind River Range. They avoided riding over rises that would skyline them, and their cook fires were kept small and sheltered.

At night, Two Buffalo rode out, looking for any sign of the Crow. The next morning, he told Tom that there had been fires to the south of them. He doubted it was the Crow. It was probably a wagon train of emigrants.

The two men rode out before daylight the next day. They chewed on jerky and drank water for their meal. Their horses or the mule would be aware of any trouble before Tom or Two Buffalo. They watched them for any indication.

Despite their precautions, a Crow appeared, astride a white horse directly in front of them as they approached the north side of the pass. The wind blew the tail and mane of the animal. Pulling their animals to a stop, Tom gripped his Hawken, ready to do battle. At any moment, he expected other braves to sweep down around them.

The Crow on the horse held his hand up, palm toward the men. "It is the sign of friendship," Two Buffalo said. "He wants to talk. You stay here and I will go."

"If he makes a hostile move toward you, I will shoot him off his horse," Tom promised.

Tom watched his friend ride out to meet with the Crow. The sun was bright in the blue sky. A breeze caused the tall grass to wave. The world around them was at peace for the moment. That could all change in an instant. The Crow calling the meeting could be looking for their horses and the trappers. Disappointment from Two Buffalo's answers could be all it took.

Sitting and watching in the hot sun, Tom could feel the sweat running down his cheeks and back. Two Buffalo and the Crow were only a few feet apart, using sign and whatever words they had in common. Tom strained his ears for any sound around him, fearful that he was being stalked.

Finally, the Crow pulled his horse around and galloped away. Tom squinted, watching for any signal from Two Buffalo. The old chief remained on the paint, staring straight ahead. After the Crow disappeared beyond a rise, Two Buffalo turned the paint and waved for Tom to join him.

Tom rode to meet the chief, leading the mule, his Hawken at the ready. He stopped beside Two Buffalo and waited. "He was one of the Crow leaders," the chief said. "The attack on the post was done by a small band of braves that are unhappy with the Crow working with the whites. He promised us we would not be bothered."

Relieved with the news, Tom was still concerned about whether the Crow leader could prevent the renegade braves from coming after them. They rode east until after dark. Tom wanted to put as much distance between the Crow camp and them as possible.

For the next several days they passed two wagon trains heading west. They spent the night with one train, getting news from the east and cautioning the emigrants about the Crow. The prairie grass had turned gold by the time they arrived back at the fort. Tom's clothing was stiff with sweat and covered with dust.

The sun was high as they tied up at the rail in front of Louie's. Tom tried to brush off some of the dust before walking in. He saw Eva arranging goods toward the back of the room. Seeing him, she squealed with joy and ran into his arms. Holding her close, he could feel the softness of her body next to him.

Louie came over, breaking up the moment, his hand outstretched, "Welcome back. I suppose you're going to take this good little worker away from me."

"It is my intention," Tom replied.

The rest of the afternoon was a frenzy of activity. Two Buffalo, who had put off going to visit his people, left after picking up a few supplies. Eva promised Louie that she would finish with the goods while Tom took care of the horses.

After making arrangements with the hostler to store the packs and give the horse and mule a good rubdown, Tom hurried back to the trading post. Ducking through the doorway into the dim interior, Tom looked but didn't see his wife. Louie called him over to the bar and set a glass of rye and a bottle in front of him.

"Eva went to the boarding house to heat some water for your bath. I promised to send you to her straight away," he said. "That is, after you tell me about your trip."

Tom gave the proprietor a quick summary of the trip, including saving Chess and Avery from the Crow. Both of the men had done business with Louie in the past and he was pleased to hear that they were alright. While they shared the rye, other men started to come in, wanting to hear about the trip.

"I got a bath getting cold and a bride waiting," Tom said. "Tomorrow I will tell you all about the trip." With that, he thanked them and headed for the boarding house.

He found Eva in the back. She had just finished filling the wooden tub that looked like a large half of a barrel. She helped him remove his clothing. Once he was in the warm water, Eva took a cloth and began washing his back, her fingers tracing some of the scars left from past battles.

"I have been thinking about something and would like to know what you think of it," he said.

"If it's about me getting in the tub with you, there isn't room," she kidded him.

Chuckling, he said, "Not that it wouldn't be a good idea, but that's not it. Last winter I trapped north of the fort. It had a cabin that needs some work. If we went up there now, I could have the place in good shape for winter. That way we would be together."

Holding the towel open for her husband, Tom climbed out of the bath. Eva gently dried his muscular frame. Impatient for a reply, Tom took her in his arms and asked, "What do you think of my idea?"

Holding him close, she kissed him. "You want to know what I think?" Expectantly, he waited. She whispered in his ear, "I think that is a fine idea."